D1235222

SWANN

BROTHERHOOD PROTECTORS WORLD

REGAN BLACK

Twisted Page Press LLC

BROTHERHOOD PROTECTORS

ORIGINAL SERIES BY ELLE JAMES

Brotherhood Protectors Series

Montana SEAL (#1)

Bride Protector SEAL (#2)

Montana D-Force (#3)

Cowboy D-Force (#4)

Montana Ranger (#5)

Montana Dog Soldier (#6)

Montana SEAL Daddy (#7)

Montana Ranger's Wedding Vow (#8)

Montana SEAL Undercover Daddy (#9)

Cape Cod SEAL Rescue (#10)

Montana SEAL Friendly Fire (#11)

Montana SEAL's Mail-Order Bride (#12)

SEAL Justice (#13)

Ranger Creed (#14)

Delta Force Rescue (#15)

Montana Rescue (Sleeper SEAL)

Hot SEAL Salty Dog (SEALs in Paradise)

Hot SEAL Hawaiian Nights (SEALs in Paradise)

Hot SEAL Bachelor Party (SEALs in Paradise)

Brotherhood Protectors World
Guardian Agency: Swann
By Regan Black

As always, with special thanks to Elle James for inviting
me into her world of
Brotherhood Protectors.

ABOUT GUARDIAN AGENCY: SWANN
When hope is lost, truth is blurred, and your life is on
the line, it's time to call
the Guardian Agency...

A dangerous thief is closing in and she is all alone...
Michelle Korbel is slowly recovering from the emotional
blow of a miscarriage following one passionate night
with the man of her dreams. Now her antique store, her
sole pride and joy, is threatened by a man convinced she
has his property.

Can a friend from her past rescue her in time?
Nolan Swann, an attorney based in Chicago, is on his way to Kansas on behalf of a client. Close enough to his home town, he'll also settle an estate for his family after avoiding the task for the past year. And he'll finally see the friend he fell into bed with once and never called again.

When Swann discovers Michelle hiding on his family property, he vows to make things right between them. But until she decides to trust him, they don't stand a chance against the thief hunting her.

Visit ReganBlack.com for a full list of books, excerpts and upcoming release dates.
For early access to new releases, exclusive prizes, and much more,
subscribe to Regan's monthly newsletter.

CHAPTER 1

MOST DAYS there was a low undercurrent of productive energy pulsing through the elegantly decorated law offices of Gamble and Swann. The Michigan Avenue address and the building centered on Chicago's Magnificent Mile were as exclusive as the clientele. On this early June afternoon the office had gone quiet on purpose. Nolan Swann and his partner, Patrick Gamble, had cleared out everyone for an important quarterly meeting with their primary client.

Although the firm employed attorneys who specialized in corporate and family law, Gamble and Swann handled criminal cases when asked to do so by the man they represented, the man who made it possible for them to pick and choose the rest of their caseload with care.

Their client wouldn't show up in person. As far as Swann knew, the man never left his estate. But even with a conference call they ruthlessly protected his privacy. So it was just the two of them in the conference room when the phone rang. After a brief greeting, they gave their quarterly report on the status of his business interests, including the current cases handled by his pet project known as the Guardian Agency.

The protection and security service didn't advertise, picking up assignments across the country solely by word of mouth. Still, they'd grown a superb reputation for stepping in and salvaging apparently lost causes.

"You did a fine job for Billie Hamilton in Montana," their client said, pride coming across loud and clear in his rusty voice. "She can't say enough good things about the agency."

"That's great news," Gamble replied evenly.

Swann glanced across the table. Billie, the U.S. Attorney in Montana, was Gamble's ex-wife. Though his partner didn't talk about her much, he'd been relieved they could help her when a high-profile case went off the rails.

"Swann, are you still worried about staffing?"

"Yes, sir, I am." He waited a beat, got Gamble's nod, and continued. "With the rate we are accepting cases, I think we could be more efficient with another analyst on board."

"Did the search for that last witness in the Native Mob case in Montana burn out Tyler completely?"

"No, sir," Gamble interjected. "He's back up to full speed."

"Good." The client cleared his throat. "I like that boy."

Swann exchanged a smile with Gamble. Their top client was an eccentric recluse, but he genuinely cared about the men and women involved with the Guardian Agency.

"And Claudia is well?"

"Yes sir," Swann said. "She's seven months along now and feeling great according to Nathan."

"Wonderful news. Make sure we set up a trust for the child."

Gamble flipped to a clean sheet on his notepad and they verified the specifics.

"Swann," the client said, when the trust was set. "I see your point. It would be nice to have another analyst in place before Claudia's maternity leave.

With that in mind, there's a young man recently sentenced to twelve years in Leavenworth. I believe he's the right analyst to add to our team. Of course, the final decision is yours, gentlemen. As always."

With a swift round of good-byes, Gamble and Swann were left staring at each other.

"He can't mean—"

"Connor Brady," Swann finished for him. "That's exactly who he's suggesting." He turned his tablet to show his partner the email that had just come through.

Gamble whistled. "If he's so good at all things IT-related, why did he get caught?"

"Clearly, we don't have all the facts." Brady had been court-martialed and found guilty of uploading top secret documents to an open-access cloud service in an attempt to sell the files. "We've successfully recruited from prisons before."

"Protectors, investigators, not analysts," Gamble protested. "How can we trust a man the U.S. Army locked up for a national security breach? He has the skills to tear up our systems, blow all our hard-won privacy measures."

Swann stared at his normally unflappable partner. Gamble, with his serious blue eyes and perfectly styled dark hair could walk into a courtroom and give a judge second thoughts about who was in control. The trouble in Montana had rattled him and it showed up at the strangest times. Like this one.

"He's never steered us wrong," Swann reminded him, tapping the speaker in the middle of the table.

Gamble paced in front of the floor-to-ceiling windows, his expression as stormy as the clouds gathering over the lake. "Even if we decide Brady is both innocent and capable of loyalty," Gamble ranted, "how do we get him out of a military prison? Overturning this particular conviction is a big ask."

"What if we try the expert consultant angle?" Swann suggested. "There's precedent for that, even at Leavenworth."

"I don't know," Gamble grumbled. "I'd like a face to face. And a look at his record since he's been inside."

"Agreed." Swann stood, loosening his tie and unbuttoning his collar. "I'll take care of that while you comb the law library."

"You *want* to go to Kansas?" Gamble eyed him with outright suspicion. "Since when?"

His partner posed a valid question. He'd been avoiding going back home since his great aunt Ellen Sue's funeral about a year ago. "I can't keep neglecting my great aunt's house while the family debates what to do with it. The neighbors cleared out the limbs that came down in the ice storm a couple months ago, but my mom volunteered me to make the repairs to the porch."

Gamble snorted. "Nice of her."

"It happens." Swann shrugged. There was another reason he wanted to get back, but that was too personal to share right now when the mention of Gamble's ex had stressed him out. "Two birds, one stone," Swann said. "As long as you're okay with me being gone for at least a week."

"Take two," Gamble replied. "I can manage."

Swann hoped it wouldn't take him that long. "Only if I have to. We'll save on expenses since I can stay at her place rather than a hotel."

"Please." Gamble rolled his eyes. "Don't act like we're just starting out. Wait. Does the place have internet?"

Swann chuckled at the old jab. "Indoor plumbing too. It's eastern Kansas, not the moon."

"Kind of the same, thing." Gamble rocked back

on his heels. "If I recall, her place wasn't exactly in the center of the action."

"That lack of action is called farming. It requires lots of space to keep this country fed." As much as he'd loved the wide open spaces of the Midwest and growing up in a small home town, once he was out, returns were rare. The last time he'd been back, for Ellen Sue's memorial service, he'd felt exposed and detached.

And his solution to rebuild that sense of belonging and connection—hooking up with his friend, Michelle—had been unwise. An amazing and fun night, but not at all the smart move. Hell, he hadn't even called her after, which meant he could only wonder now about how she was doing.

Would she be interested in spending some more time together? Most likely she'd moved on, found some great local guy to build a future with. One night stand or not, he should've called.

Irritated by his misgivings over things he couldn't control, he walked out of the conference room. In his office, he gathered up his laptop and essential papers while he and Gamble briefly debated practical approaches to reversing Connor Brady's sentence.

"I'll dig into the research," Gamble promised,

"But I want your take on this guy before we invest too much time and effort."

Swann paused at the door. "We have our instructions."

"We also have final say on our personnel."

"Why does this spook you?" he asked.

His partner raked a hand through his dark hair. "It was nearly treason," Gamble said through clenched teeth. "The man dropped files in what amounted to a cloud exchange for national secrets."

Swann understood the frustration. Loyalty was paramount for Gamble. For both of them, really. But working from their client's guidance, they had cultivated the best people for the Guardian Agency. The men and women who came on board were rarely from pristine backgrounds. Life wasn't that neat and tidy. But so far their success rate with personnel was one hundred percent.

"He wouldn't be the first innocent person accused and convicted," Swann pointed out. "Not even the first we've hired." They'd met in law school—more specifically in the law library— during a summer internship with a legal team dedicated to clearing prisoners who had been wrongly convicted.

"I know, I know." Gamble cracked his knuckles and stepped aside so Swann could head out. "Just be careful."

"Always." Well almost always. He hadn't been all that careful with Michelle. "Between the two of us, we'll figure out if Brady fits the agency."

Gamble's reservations followed Swann on the short drive north to his condo in the Gold Coast neighborhood. They'd planted the law firm here, at their benefactor's request, so they would be within easy reach of clients across the nation. Today was proof they'd made the right call, he thought as he put in the flight request with the firm's private jet service. He continued working through his to-do list, booking a rental car, sending an email head's up to the closest neighbor to his great aunt's house. It was a pleasant surprise to realize he could place a grocery order online for pick up. It seemed the small town of Leavenworth, Kansas had entered the twenty-first century.

By the time he'd called the prison for a meeting and scheduled the car service for transportation to the airport, he was feeling almost eager to head back to his roots.

CHAPTER 2

MICHELLE KORBEL LOCKED the front door and turned out all the lights except for the one over the display window that faced Delaware Street at the front of her antique store. Walking to her office in the back, she passed various displays, relishing the sweet satisfaction of another solid day doing business in Leavenworth's historic district.

She'd counted the cash drawer for the deposit she would drop off in the morning, but she still had some paperwork to finish for another online auction and emails to respond to before she could call it a day. On a normal day, she would take her laptop home to handle those details, with music or a movie on in the background.

Nothing felt normal since she'd found signs of

an attempted break-in around her back door at home a few days ago. Between the close-knit neighbors on her street and the warm, small-town vibe of Leavenworth, it had seemed overkill to install a security system at home, despite the prisons in the area. Filing a report with the police department hadn't made her feel better, so she'd installed a security system she could monitor through her cell phone.

And still, she stayed right here, avoiding going home to an empty house. Or worse, a robbery in progress.

It wasn't as if she didn't have plenty to do here and leftovers from her lunch in the refrigerator to see her through if she got hungry. Dealing with the last of her paperwork, she opened her store email. An increasing percentage of her business was conducted online directly through her website and people regularly inquired about pieces she had in the store as well.

She opened an email about an armoire she'd recently acquired and mentally crossed her fingers. It was a sizable piece, in excellent condition and highly photogenic. Her bubble of excitement over a potential sale burst as the tone of the email became clear.

Not again. This was the second email in the past three days regarding the lot that included the armoire. A member of the family claimed the piece had been sold to the auction house in error. Naturally, they wanted the armoire returned to the family at the earliest opportunity. They'd even provided an address and requested priority shipping.

She snorted. As if she was in the habit of sending out stock because someone on the other side of an email address requested it. She wasn't about to validate the email with a reply. With a couple of clicks, she tucked the email into a folder where she kept similar requests, just in case something came through that she did need to take action on.

The auction house shouldn't have given out her contact information as the buyer, but sometimes people made a good guess or did their homework through online searches. Or the auction house had simply let something slip.

But now the shop didn't feel safe either. Definitely not when the other stores were closed. She shut down her laptop and slipped it into her tote. As she reached for the light switch, she heard the handle on the door to the alley rattle.

Her shop was wired for security with a silent alarm that went straight to the police station, same as most of the shops in this part of town. In addition to the sensors at the doors, there was an emergency button near the cash register and sensors on the front windows too.

She moved back into her office and turned the lock. In the dark she fumbled a moment, but found her cell phone and called 911. The dispatcher answered just as cool air flowed under the office door. Someone had opened the back door.

Holding her breath she waited until the footsteps passed, rubber soles barely audible on the polished concrete flooring. She whispered her name and address. "Someone is inside," she said, praying that person was too distracted to hear her.

The next sound was a crash, followed by a faint siren growing closer. Michelle huddled in the corner. Her thoughts raced from the near break-in to the emails to this actual break-in. It couldn't be coincidence. She'd heard stories of people going to great lengths when they'd lost an item with significant sentimental or monetary value. It must just be her turn.

The owner of those rubber-soled shoes ran by

the office and when the police arrived, calling her name, the burglar was gone.

Officer Quinn, a petite blond woman with soft blue eyes in a heart-shaped face that belied her toughness and years of experience with the Leavenworth PD took her statement, walked through the store with her assessing the damage.

"Is anything obvious missing?" Quinn asked, glancing around.

There was no obvious purpose to the break-in. A glass-fronted bookcase had absorbed the burglar's fall when he apparently tripped on an area rug, but none of the items were missing, only broken. "Everything's accounted for." Mentally, she added a call to her insurance company to her to-do list for tomorrow.

She hated to give voice to her weakness and the growing fear, but she really didn't want to be here alone if the person returned. "Would you mind sticking around while I clean up the worst of it?"

Quinn smiled. "Take your time, Michelle." Her gaze drifted toward a display of quilts. "I can keep myself busy," she said with a wink. The woman loved quilting when she wasn't keeping the peace.

Once the police were done with pictures and fingerprints, Michelle used her cell phone to document the damage for her insurance adjuster. The book case could be salvaged, once the glass was replaced, but new glass diminished the overall value. Maybe she'd keep it for display purposes only.

Quinn walked her all the way to her car and promised to keep an officer on patrol until the lock could be changed tomorrow. Probably not a bad idea to post another do-it-yourself system here. Just as another layer of protection. A device like that would have given the police a view of the would-be burglar.

Her hands trembled as she started the car. Where to go? She didn't want to go home, didn't want to be alone at any address that was part of the public record. Thankfully, she always had an overnight bag in the trunk, so she didn't have to go home at all. Considering the limited options in town, she aimed for the highway and a client she'd been neglecting for too long.

Ellen Sue Howell had been an icon in Leavenworth and as a community everyone was missing her since her death just over a year ago. Her home, a beautiful testament to craftsmanship, was planted in the middle of prime farmland west of town. She'd been leasing the land for nearly three

REGAN BLACK

decades and collecting various antiques for even
longer. The family had asked Michelle to give
them an appraisal and advice, though there hadn't
been any hurry to do a full inventory. Since her
funeral, someone from the family had been stopping in every few months to collect the pieces of
her life that mattered to them.

In the past six months, Michelle had seen all of
Ellen Sue's relatives except the man she most
wanted to see, Nolan Swann. Just the thought of
the sexy lawyer eased some of the tension gathered
across her shoulders. Ellen Sue had introduced
them and he'd been an unexpected friend when
she'd first established her store.

She'd practically tripped over her tongue at
that first meeting. He'd come back to town to do
some work for Ellen Sue and the surrounding
farmers in the summer before he started law
school. His dark blond hair had been pushed back
from his face, and the golden scruff sparkled on
his jaw from days without shaving. A sweat-soaked
shirt had clung to his muscled torso as he scraped
shingles off a roof. He'd paused in his task long
enough to smile at his great aunt and wave hello to
Michelle. Oh, the man had a smile that could melt
ice. It was a sweet and happy memory and the first

of a summer flirtation they'd both enjoyed that had never gone further than a few nights of dancing and a couple of amazing kisses.

So she resisted the guilt in her stomach for going to hide in a house that wasn't really hers, though it had always felt like a second home. She'd start on the inventory tonight. To validate her choice. Working beat worrying about troubling emails and burglars.

As she drove out of town, she checked her mirror time and again as fear took root deep between her shoulder blades. With minimal traffic out this way she would soon know if she'd been followed. Then again, there were only so many roads between town and the surrounding farms. She kept her thumb over the hands-free calling option, just in case.

As she turned off the highway and the motion lights spaced along the winding drive winked on, she wondered if she could possibly afford to buy the place from the Swann family. Already her breathing eased. She paused in front of the house, her headlights winking off the front windows and door. She would happily upgrade to this big farm house from her cottage in town. Sure, her place was closer to her store, but the quiet and solitude out here gave her such a sense of peace. A mental break.

Despite the lack of near neighbors, thanks to Ellen Sue's longstanding leases for the fields, trustworthy farmers were in the area all the time. Michelle parked her car in the barn-turned-garage. Gathering her purse, computer bag and overnight case, Michelle walked the stone path to the house, the shrubs and flowers making the short trek a treat for the senses, even at twilight. The family had someone to keep up with the house, but as things greened up after winter, Michelle had started coming out to tend the garden beds.

Overhead in a melting gray sky, stars winked into view as the last of the light faded. The sadness that had plagued her in recent months was muted here. Pulling out her key, she let herself into the backdoor and stepped inside.

A hint of furniture polish and the mint tea Ellen Sue preferred before bed lingered in the air, even a year later. Michelle caught herself before calling out a greeting for her old friend. She carried her things straight into the kitchen and set the kettle on to boil water. Mint tea would be a comfort after the way her day ended.

While the tea steeped, she set up her computer

in the den in the back of the house, keeping the lights to a soothing low. One wall was devoted to built-in cabinetry, packed with books from classics to contemporary cozy mysteries and antique tea pots that ran the gamut from elegant to whimsical. A few Michelle had acquired for her friend. The furniture was bulky and inviting and the windows overlooked the fields behind the house. In the daytime it was a stunning, wide-open view that stretched to the horizon.

She prepared to finish the work interrupted by the attempted burglary, but yet another email from the same unhappy sender was just too much. It wasn't her first run in with seller's remorse and it wouldn't be the last, but the tone and the persistence made her edgy.

She closed the device and walked away. Cell phone in one hand, tea in the other, she started cataloguing Ellen Sue's furnishings. This room held the majority of the woman's collection of teapots. There were a few empty spaces from pieces that had been handed down in the year since the funeral, but several remaining would bring a high price at auction.

Being proactive calmed her as nothing else, restoring her sense of control. Her tea went cold as she worked her way through the first floor, taking pictures and notes. Her excitement grew as she returned to her computer to start on the preliminary search for comparable items and estimated values. The family couldn't have any idea what the contents of the house were worth to the right buyer.

It was well-past midnight when she took her suitcase upstairs to one of the guest rooms. Dragging, she slid under the covers and set the alarm on her phone. Tomorrow would be busy with appointments and resetting the store.

She'd barely dozed off when an alert chirped. Sitting up, she checked the display and wished she hadn't. Not an email this time, a text message. And this hadn't been forwarded from the store number, but sent directly to her personal cell phone.

you will return my property

The sender was listed only as 'unknown'. Maybe it was a mistake, but she sent a screenshot to Quinn just in case.

Then she tiptoed down the hall for the shotgun and shells Ellen Sue kept in her bedroom closet, returning to her room to wait for the morning.

SWANN LEFT THE PRISON, grateful he had the option, and strode purposefully to his rental car. Maybe he should've listened to Gamble's misgivings and just said no to Connor Brady. But he'd been stubborn about backing their top client.

At the car, he tossed his briefcase to the passenger seat and managed not to pummel the steering wheel while he called his partner. He missed the buzz of life in Chicago. The quiet and wide open views broken with an occasional stand of trees were grating on him already.

Getting the runaround at the prison didn't help matters.

"How'd it go?" Gamble asked when he came on the line.

"I'm not sure yet," Swann admitted. "The warden wasn't too pleased to see me and Brady didn't help matters by rejecting the meeting."

"What the hell is that about?"

"I'm not sure yet. I got in there, but it was some quick talking. Thankfully, the kid is more curious than resigned to his conviction."

"Is he innocent?" Gamble queried.

"I'm sure of it," Swann replied without hesitation.

"All right. I'll put in more effort on the research

side. So far I haven't found much of a legal precedent."

Swann knew his partner had a thumb pressed hard to his temple, thinking of the pros, cons and all possible outcomes. There was no doubt in his mind Brady had been railroaded or possibly coerced into pleading guilty. No surprise really, the mind and money behind the Guardian Agency didn't steer them towards bad seeds, only those who look bad on paper.

This kid looked dreadful on paper. "He has the skills we need and the temperament too. I think he fits in with our agency goals."

"You've read through the depositions, right?" Gamble asked. "The case is locked up tight. No judge wants to overturn a national security conviction."

True. "But everyone wants to be the hero and see justice served to the right offender. I've combed his personnel record. This kid had been with his unit less than a year when they slapped cuffs on him. He followed orders twenty-four-seven and was top of his class practically since the day he stepped into the recruiting office."

"Even good soldiers make mistakes," Gamble grumbled.

Also true. "He's a scapegoat," Swann insisted. Gut deep he was sure of that. "Somehow we have to prove it and sooner rather than later. He's afraid of something or, more accurately, someone."

"Of course he is, he's in Leavenworth for a minimum of twelve years."

"Something on the outside," Swann clarified. "When was the last time he was wrong?" Swann challenged, referring to their top client.

Gamble's heavy sigh was answer enough. "What's next on your list for Brady?"

"I'll dig into the chain of command. The person responsible for dropping that virtual hard drive into an unsecured bucket on the cloud is higher up the food chain."

"Be careful," Gamble said. "If we tip our hand too early we blow it for Brady and us."

Swann agreed. "I'd like to talk to Hank Patterson." The former SEAL ran his own security and protection agency out of Montana and had collaborated with them on the search for three protected witnesses who had been exposed during the case Hamilton had been prosecuting. "We know he can be discreet." And Swann hoped he could put him in touch with someone who had a more objective view of the key players in Brady's case.

"I'll pass it along that we've reached out and are proceeding as asked," Gamble said. "But I think this one could take some time."

"Unless he recants his story and we can find a way to back it up, you're right about that," Swann agreed. "Any updates on our other cases?" he asked.

"You missing the routine already?" Gamble chuckled. "It's barely been twenty-four hours. Claudia tells me our protector made contact. That's all I know right now."

"Well here's hoping we have smooth sailing for a while. Our team could use a break after that mess in Montana."

"Danger and risk is often why our bodyguards sign on," Gamble reminded him.

"Knowing the risks to our team and liking those risks are two different things. It will take me some time before I stop worrying about retaliation."

"How's the house?" Gamble asked, changing the subject.

"No idea. I came straight to the prison," Swann replied. "I plan to drop by my favorite diner and maybe do a little more research before I pick up my grocery order."

"So, you're avoiding it."

"I like to think it's a matter of prioritizing and focus. We have a kid who needs our help and his situation is more urgent. The house isn't going anywhere."

"You really miss her," Gamble said.

He leaped to defend himself, realizing in the nick of time that his partner was referencing his great aunt, not Michelle. Sneaking away for hours in bed with her had been a bright distraction after the horrendously emotional day of memorial services and shared family grief.

"We all do," he managed, needing to say something. "I told my mom about this trip, that I'd take care of a few repairs too, and she reminded me the family wants me to decide the fate of the house."

"Will you sell or save it for the next generation?"

Swann snorted. His gaze roaming across the barren landscape flanking the prison. It wasn't as if Leavenworth was a vacation hot spot. The area boasted rural beauty and quiet-life benefits, but to live out here? He couldn't see it, not after seeing other parts of the world and thriving in Chicago. "We'll see." Arranging to sell meant taking care of the repairs, negotiating the fields and access for the farmers leasing that land. It also meant speaking with Michelle about the value of Ellen Sue's collections.

And there it was, the spark of hope that this visit might not have to be all business.

Swann swapped one conversation for the next, dialing Hank's number. Through the years, Patterson had built his Brotherhood Protectors into a well-respected, multi-faceted private security firm. Thanks to Claudia's connections, the Guardian Agency had recently collaborated with Hank's team on a few sensitive cases and Swann was a big fan of the new rapport. Every good resource was important.

The voice mail picked up at Hank's office and Swann left a message requesting a simple call back. No way would he give details on this case over the phone. With one last assessment of the prison he would be visiting frequently in the days ahead, he started the car and headed into town.

He drove into Leavenworth proper and his mouth watered at the mere thought of a meatloaf sandwich from Plum's diner. He could fill up, plan out the interviews he hoped to set up in the next few days, and then grab his grocery order on his way to his great aunt's place.

And as a bonus, the diner was across the street from Michelle's antiques store. With a few casual questions he was likely to get the background he needed on her current situation before he made a fool of himself. He might be feeling guilty about not calling her for no reason. She'd probably moved on with her life, never giving him another thought.

His stomach cramped, though he had no right to object to that possible outcome.

From what his mother had told him during their chat on his drive from the airport this morning, the house was in good shape overall. The utilities were still on, the bills paid from the estate finances, and someone came in from time to time to keep things clean for potential showings. The locals knew the family planned to sell, as long as it was the right buyer. Ideas had floated around about turning the property into a camp of some sort or even a bed and breakfast, but Swann didn't see it happening. Maybe he'd feel different once he got out there.

It sounded as if the family had removed the items of sentimental value, leaving him with the matter of preparing for the next step. Whatever that was.

In the diner, he was greeted by friendly faces, most of which he recognized and all of whom welcomed him back. A year ago everyone in the community had gathered for a celebration of his great aunt's life. Ellen Sue had been the last of his family in the area and they considered her a local treasure for the way she stayed involved, kept up traditions, and instigated various charitable efforts.

While the services had been gut-wrenching, the outpouring of affection had been heartwarming. Overwhelmed, Swann had gone out for a breather and ended up taking a walk with Michelle, sharing memories and laughs. He'd never been able to pinpoint when the mood had shifted, but a comforting hug had lit a fire under his skin. Then she'd let him kiss her under a deepening sky and they'd wound up at her place. It had been an unforgettable night that he never should've ignored.

Michelle had been there when he needed a distraction and a life-affirming connection. They had both fallen into that bed with eyes wide open and no promises implied. Still, a man with any decency would've called.

Across the street, he noticed her shop was

closed despite the posted hours. The three men who populated the corner booth for as far back as Swann could remember told him about the break-in the night before. Everyone in the diner was thankful she hadn't been injured and they were all equally curious if the police would find the culprit.

He fell into the rhythm of his home town, chatting about acquaintances and local news and speculating on the pricing trends of corn and wheat while he waited for a spaghetti dinner to take with him.

It was a short drive to the grocery store and his cell phone rang in his pocket as he walked out with his order. He managed to juggle the load just enough to answer. "Nolan Swann, how may I help you?"

"Hey, it's Hank returning your call. You guys doing okay?"

"All good here." Swann didn't want to discuss this out in the open any more than he wanted to leave sensitive details in a voice message. "Give me a second to get to my car. I have some questions that are best kept private."

"You said something along those lines right before we were up to our elbows with a nasty gang."

"Can't claim this isn't nasty." Swann put the groceries on the floor behind the driver's seat and then settled behind the wheel. "Thanks for your patience. Do you know anything about the Army v. Connor Brady case?"

Hank made a strange sound. "Isn't he the one who left sensitive documents on the cloud for a foreign agency to pick up at will?"

"That's the case," Swann said. "I'm just not sure Brady is the guilty party."

"U.S. Army sure thought so," Hank pointed out. "Do I want to know why you're looking into it?"

Swann wasn't about to reveal how the Guardian Agency recruited their personnel. "Favor for a friend," he said. "My first interview with Brady raised all kinds of questions. Any chance you know anyone with an opinion on the officers in Brady's chain of command?"

Hank whistled low. "I've been out a good long time, but I'll ask around. We have a few new faces who were on joint operations and might have an opinion."

"All I ask is discretion," Swann said, relieved by even that hint of help on this.

"And you'll get it," Hank promised. "That's one sticky mess I don't want to be affiliated with at all."

"Understood," Swann said. "But if the evidence put the wrong man behind bars I would feel like crap leaving him there."

Ending the call, Swann drove out to Ellen Sue's place, wondering why he was so willing to believe in Brady while Hank and Gamble maintained reservations. Yes, the case was tricky, but they'd never been asked to interview or consider taking on a guilty criminal.

And he just didn't believe that was the case here, though it would be nice to know why the man they represented believed so much in a kid he couldn't possibly have met. Falling down that rabbit hole wasn't smart and could only result in a dead end. Privacy and distance were paramount with their top client to protect everyone involved.

CHAPTER 3

MICHELLE HAD SPENT the next day running around. Into town for the bank deposit and for meetings with the police and her insurance adjuster. The store remained closed, following Officer Quinn's advice after they discussed the text message along with the previous emails. The police would work the break-in and all she could do was wait. In the meantime, she and Crystal, her part-time assistant at the store, cleaned up the damage and reset the displays so they could reopen tomorrow on schedule.

In light of the threats, Officer Quinn had asked Michelle and her adjuster to examine the rest of the items in the lot from the auction house, in case something *had* arrived in error. Only the armoire had made it to the store, everything else was at the climate-controlled storage unit on the south side of town waiting to be photographed and assessed for placement at the store or direct sale online.

The delivery from the auction house in Oklahoma included a traditional secretary desk with a hutch, a cane desk chair and a standing jewelry chest along with several vintage brooches, none of which were appraised at more than twenty dollars. The first email referenced a smaller jewelry box sent by mistake in one of the armoire drawers. She and her adjuster had searched through everything and come up empty. The upset seller had to be mistaken about when and where the jewelry box had gone.

She'd gone home to pack for an extended stay at Ellen Sue's only to realize too late that someone had been watching her house. A white compact car had pulled up behind her at a four-way stop and stayed on her tail ever since. She couldn't lead trouble to her only safe place left, so she kept driving west as she called for help.

Michelle battled wave after wave of anxiety, expecting the worst as she reported the white car to the LPD who transferred the call to the sheriff's department. The dispatcher instructed her to stop at the next gas station and wait inside for assistance.

Finding the designated gas station, she pulled in and took the first open space near the door. With her phone in one hand and keys in the other, she dashed inside as the white car drove on by.

Was she letting exhaustion overwhelm common sense?

Fortunately, the deputy sheriff didn't blow off her claim of being followed, taking her concerns seriously and even escorting her to the turn off for Ellen Sue's place. Once her car was safely out of sight in the barn, Michelle started to breathe easy. She decided to change clothes and work outside in the flowers. It would be a healthy and productive way to pull herself together and she could have fresh-cut flowers on the table for dinner.

Two hours later, she sat on the back porch with a glass of hard lemonade and the pleasant ache of hard work in her hands. She watched the early evening breeze stir the rows of growing corn beyond the old tractor. Occasionally a car or truck rumbled by on the state road that served as the western border of the property and she braced for the worst until the sound faded.

She'd brought the shotgun downstairs this

morning, stashing it near the front door and propping a baseball bat at the back door. If anyone approached, she would have time to get inside and take up a weapon if needed. She couldn't stay out here indefinitely, but surely the LPD or the sheriff's department would have a lead soon.

Her cell phone buzzed with an alert. Someone had tripped the sensor at her house. Well away from the danger, Michelle's temper flared with this new threat. It looked like a man, but she couldn't tell because of how he kept his head down, and a ball cap pulled low. Through the app, she immediately reported the problem to the LPD. Changing to the view from the doorbell camera out front, she spotted that blasted white car.

Though the problem was miles away, Michelle felt too exposed outside. She needed to clean up anyway. Heading inside, she locked the doors and took the shotgun upstairs to shower and change before figuring out what to do about dinner.

Dressed in soft leggings and a loose tee, she braided her damp hair back from her face and headed downstairs to the kitchen. She was in the pantry when she heard a car engine and it was all she could do not to turn out the lights. But that would alert whoever was out there that someone was inside.

She moved through the dark front room, and peeked through the lace curtain. It wasn't the white car in the driveway, but no one else should be here and she didn't recognize the vehicle. Dark blue or black, it was hard to tell in the evening light, the sedan screamed luxury. Far too nice to belong to any of the neighboring farmers. Was more than one person tracking down the item she didn't actually have?

Reaching for the shotgun, she realized she'd left it upstairs. Her cell phone too. This far out it would take the police too long to respond anyway. Cursing herself, she tiptoed back to the kitchen for the baseball bat. She would *not* go down without a fight.

She heard the hinges on the screen door squeak and protest, then a key in the lock. Was this a realtor, checking on the place for a potential buyer? If it had been anyone from the family, they would've called her or sent an email as a head's up.

Holding her ground in the dark corner just outside the kitchen, she waited, planning how she would strike, how much of a head start she needed to get to the garage and get away.

The screen door squeaked and slapped closed. Lights came on in the front room, then the hallway. The footsteps paused at the kitchen. She expected to hear sounds of a search, instead it sounded more like someone was putting groceries away. The refrigerator door kept opening and closing, cabinets bumped closed. Weird.

At the sound of paper bags being folded, she lunged through the doorway, using the bat like a battering ram. The man turned around and she drove the bat into his gut. He fell back, into the cast iron sink. The impact knocked the air from his lungs and he crumpled to the floor, his head rapping against the sink's edge. His eyes bulged as he tried to speak, then he curled into himself, gasping for air. Only then did she really look at him and as his features registered, she panicked.

"Oh my God! Nolan. What are you doing here?"

Unfortunately, he couldn't answer in his current condition. His face was turning red, his hands were covering his middle and he stared at her with shock and confusion in his sky-blue eyes. She dropped the bat and crouched beside him, hands fluttering all over that handsome face around his neck, gingerly searching for injury.

"I'm so sorry." Wouldn't it be just her luck to

hurt the one man she'd wanted to see again for the past year?

He scooted out of her reach, sitting a little straighter and sipping air carefully into his lungs. "Give me a minute," he rasped. "Just a minute."

She sat back on her heels, giving him some space, but unwilling to go far. Seeing his sunglasses on the floor in the corner, she moved to pick them up. "Not broken," she said, setting them on the table.

"Good." A scowl furrowed his brow. "What the hell?"

Aside from the blow she'd delivered, he looked amazing in the gray suit and dark blue dress shirt. She went to the front door and locked it. When she returned to the kitchen, he was still on the floor, his back against the cabinets, hands resting on his up-drawn knees.

"Michelle." He squinted at her, as he took another labored breath. "Why are you here? Why —" The question was interrupted by a spate of coughing.

"I'm working on the antiques inventory," she said. "No one told me to expect you."

He nodded as if that made perfect sense. "Last

minute deal," he explained. "Business trip and personal."

Her pulse skipped. Was he including her in that personal label? Of course not. He was here to deal with his great aunt's house, not to reconnect with her.

She didn't know a lot about his business as a lawyer, but with three different prisons in the area it was logical that he might have a client in one of them. And possibly his arrival was fortuitous. She might need legal help to clear up this bogus claim on her last acquisition.

Reaching down, she helped him to his feet. Standing toe-to-toe, her body remembered everything about him. The scent of his skin drifted over her, tempted her. At five-foot-seven she wasn't exactly short, but she felt petite as she looked up to into his eyes. They were the blue of a clear October sky and full of annoyed ire at the moment. For the first time she preferred that almost shy, not quite guilty, thoroughly bewildered look he had on his face as he had kissed her goodbye and walked out of her bedroom a year ago.

"I'm sorry about jumping you and, well everything." She returned the bat to its place by the back door and poured him a glass of water. She managed to hand it over without touching him. "I wasn't expecting anyone."

"Neither was I," he said, taking small sips of water.

She couldn't stop staring at him, drinking him in. "I was alone. Working on the inventory."

He arched one of those burnished-gold eyebrows. "Can't be too careful."

"Right." Being the focal point of all that intense energy and concentration was unsettling and exhilarating.

His gaze roamed over her from head to toe and then drifted around the kitchen. "I didn't see a car outside."

"I'm parked in the barn," she explained.

"Why?"

Noticing the six-pack of beer on the counter, she put it into the refrigerator for him. That's where she saw the takeout from Plum's. "Looks like you're staying a while." And now she had to find a new safe place. She had no immediate ideas.

"I picked up the spaghetti special. There's more than enough to share if you haven't eaten."

"Smart choice," she said. She wasn't hungry for

food, just now. Comfort and distraction, she'd take big helpings of both if he offered.

He refilled his water glass and downed it swiftly before striding to the window that over-looked the fields behind the house. "So, your car is in the barn. Were you planning on staying over?"

Naturally, he wouldn't let that go. Nolan didn't like open-ended questions. "Only if the inventory kept me here late," she said. Neither her home nor the store were safe options, which left her with... where? She had no idea.

"How long will you be in town?" In addition to the beer and the takeout, she'd seen a selection of bread, meats and cheeses for sandwiches, plus a dozen eggs and a carton of milk. "A while I'm guessing." The more pressing concern was if she could keep her mouth shut about the baby she'd lost. There was no sense in blurting that out, in giving him a moment's grief or sorrow about something he couldn't change.

"Maybe a couple of weeks," he said. "The business side won't be as easy as I'd hoped, and some things need repaired around here before we can do anything with the house. I'll do my best to stay out of your way."

He could never be in her way. On her mind, but

that seemed to be the same whether he was physically present of not. She really should have put that night, and everything that followed, behind her by now. "I'll do the same. It is your house."

"But the contents are practically yours." He shrugged out of his suit coat and draped it over one of the kitchen chairs.

The crisp, deep blue shirt set off his eyes. Tailored so well, it hugged his torso and her hands tingled with the memory of untucking a similar shirt the night of the memorial.

"The estimates for the antiques and collectibles shouldn't take me more than another week after the inventory is done."

"Sounds good." His gaze didn't quite meet hers.

If she didn't know better, she'd think he was uncertain. She couldn't recall a time when Nolan had been uncomfortable in any situation. He always seemed to know exactly what to do, where to be, and how to say what needed said in any given moment.

In contrast she had absolutely no clue how to keep up a pretense that everything was fine between them. Should she pretend she'd never seen him naked? Did he expect her to ask why he'd never called? It's not like she tried calling him. It was a one-night deal and though she'd never been quite content with the notion of not seeing him again, the situation didn't feel like a problem until she'd found herself pregnant.

"You're probably mad. With good reason," he said. "I should have called," he added.

Guilt riddled her. "I could've called you." She'd been on the verge of doing so when she miscarried. At that point it seemed prudent to keep things as they'd been—a one and done night of passion to ease the grip of sorrow. There was no reason to tell him about a baby that didn't exist, then or now.

It made no sense to look at him right now and have any what-if feelings. They were from two different worlds, despite his being born and raised here. Their friendship started with Ellen Sue and it had been natural that her service made them both emotional enough to do something equally comforting and rash.

"You should eat," she said. "I'll, um, get to work upstairs."

"Actually, I stuffed myself with a meatloaf sandwich before I picked up the groceries. I'd planned to do some paperwork, but I'd rather catch up with you."

Was he blushing or was the color in his face a remnant of her attack? "That's really thoughtful. Maybe some other night." Her palms started to sweat and she wasn't even out the door. "It's your first night back in town in how long?"

His gaze narrowed and she felt like a bug under a microscope. "About a year."

"Right." Her attempt at a breezy reply came out breathless. "I've mostly been in touch with your mom, letting the family come through for the items they want."

He planted his hands on his hips. "My last visit to town wasn't memorable enough for you?"

The heat in her cheeks was too revealing as his mellow voice rolled over her. She couldn't dignify that with a reply. She walked away, aiming for the den to gather up her purse and computer. "All I'm saying is that with your schedule I assumed you'd been back and forth a time or two by now."

"I should have called," he muttered it under his breath, so low she almost didn't hear him.

She didn't want him to carry any guilt about that night. "Nolan, it is good to see you. Enjoy your time. Maybe we can talk before you go back."

"Please stay, Michelle. We are both here. Why not start the conversation tonight?"

She was caught, not wanting to leave and not comfortable staying. But pretending everything in her life was good and normal was better than trying to figure out where she could safely hide from the person who was getting too bold.

Then again if the remorseful seller found her here, she was putting Nolan at risk. Her eyes skated over him. He looked capable of handling any and all trouble. It was a heady feeling being in his presence again. "It isn't weird for you?"

"Should it be weird that I've seen you naked?" he asked with a grin and a wink.

She tried to be an adult, but she failed miserably, thoroughly overcome by giggles. It was all too much. The emails, and text message, the disturbances at the shop and her house, being followed and now standing here face to face with the man who populated her fantasies. Resistance was futile.

"You look great," he said. "Especially without the baseball bat."

"Thanks," she croaked, her throat dry. "You look great too."

"Is that a yes?" He cocked an eyebrow. "You'll stay a while and catch me up?"

"As long as we don't talk about naked things," she replied.

"Deal." His low chuckle rumbled through the outdated country kitchen and she was done for. "Do you want a beer?"

"Only if you're having one too."

He stretched his neck from side to side. "I don't know. Probably not smart if I'm nursing a concussion," he teased.

"Stop," she said, laughing. "I thought you were an intruder after those teapots."

But he didn't laugh with her. No, those expressive golden eyebrows snapped together. "You attacked me like you were expecting trouble." He lifted his chin toward the back door. "Looks like you're set for round two."

She waved that off, topping off his water glass and filling another one for herself. "A single woman out on a farm can't be too careful. Ellen Sue taught me that."

"I'm sure she wasn't the only one."

Michelle appreciated the displeasure in his voice about that truth. She'd learned to take care of herself early in life, same as most women she knew. It didn't seem to matter where you lived, if you lived alone you had to be able to handle yourself.

She wasn't handling this remorseful seller very

well so far. That needed to change. Easier to do if she understood what she was up against. Claims about having another person's property, without any specifics weren't helpful. Right now it was more fun to focus on Nolan and what had brought him back to town. "I didn't realize you represented anyone other than Ellen Sue's estate. Do you have a client nearby?"

"Basically." He drank some water and she tried to ignore the way his throat moved. "What I have is a client interested in an Army prisoner who needs help. I met with the prisoner today and can't figure out why he isn't eager to help us reverse his conviction."

"Who wants to stay in prison?"

"Right?" His eyes sparked and he pulled out a chair and sat down at the kitchen table. "I like a challenge, but I'm afraid it will take some time to sort out the details and get to the real culprit."

Some time. She wouldn't mind having Nolan around for some time. Maybe they could find something closer to a real friendship again. Or even enjoy each other more intimately. Her body craved his and feeding that addiction probably wasn't smart. She was sure it would be fun.

"You think he's protecting someone," she said,

dragging her thoughts back to the safer territory of his business here.

"Possibly even himself. My partner at the office is working on the legal research. Once we know more about the original case I'll have more to work with."

"I didn't realize you did so much criminal work," she said, taking the seat across from him at the table.

"If we did more this case might be easier for me to get my head around." He pushed his hands through his hair as he tipped his head back. "We handle a variety of legal situations," he explained. "Most of them revolve around private or civilian matters. This military situation is a special case and the client who hired us to help this kid isn't one I can say no to."

"You make your client sound like a mob boss," she said.

Nolan laughed, leaning forward to rest his elbows on the table. "That would make me a mob lawyer from Kansas and that's hysterical."

"But you live in Chicago now," she pointed out.

"Still, no." He looked around the kitchen. "Ellen Sue would've cackled over that," he said, sadly. "She had the best laugh."

"From what I heard, you haven't made your choices yet. Is there anything in particular you know you want?" she asked.

He pondered that with a flex of his brow. "Why don't we walk through the house and I'll let you know."

It was the right answer and yet it scared her. Some of the best pieces were upstairs in the bedrooms and she wasn't sure it was a good idea to be alone with Nolan near a bed. Her desire for another hot night was growing by the minute. Preferably a night without the complicated stress and worry that had followed the last time.

CHAPTER 4

NOLAN PUSHED BACK from the table wishing he could just pull Michelle in close and kiss her. Would it relieve this awkwardness or make it worse? She was so easy to be around and he wondered how he could go a year without seeing her and suddenly fall back into friendly conversation.

He supposed it said more about her than him. Michelle had a kind and generous heart. He'd known that from their first meeting on a charity home repair event his great aunt had organized. But she also had a body that didn't quit. A body he'd missed far more than he should have this past year.

Despite the easy conversation, he sensed there

was more going on with her. Something she didn't want to discuss. Thankfully, whatever was bothering her didn't seem related to their past. He wondered how to draw it out of her without overstepping.

He hadn't been himself after Ellen Sue's memorial. He needed connection and space at the same time. Michelle had offered him warmth and affection when he most needed it, expecting nothing in return.

They moved into the sitting room with a wide window overlooking the porch and the drive before it curled out of sight and he turned on the light. He remembered his great aunt sitting here entertaining her friends through the years. Sometimes they would gather out on the porch and chat about everything from the weather to the latest recipe, but if the conversation was serious or the weather lousy, they cozied up in here. The furniture and décor was formal and yet welcoming. Even when he was small he'd been invited to spend time with her in here. He never once felt as if he was too messy or too much of a little boy for the space, despite the floral upholstery, frilly throw pillows and coordinated tea service.

"Where's the tea set?" he asked, looking around

the room. The one decorated in sunflowers, her favorite, was always on the cart in the corner ready to be put to use the minute someone dropped in.

"Your mother requested that one," Michelle replied. "I sent it to her about six months ago."

Swann noticed the way she'd dipped her head, and stepped away from him as she spoke. "Was it a set you wanted to sell or keep for yourself? Ellen Sue wanted you to have whatever suited you for either purpose."

"No, I was perfectly happy to send it along," she said in a hurry.

There it was again, an uneasiness just under the surface that her smile didn't quite hide. He had years of experience interviewing clients and knew when people were distracted or lying. It was even easier for him to detect with people he cared about.

It was a little unsettling to realize she fell into the latter category. Not that he didn't care about her as a person, but they weren't exactly close. What they had—aside from the friendship—had been a matter of convenience.

"Your mom told me the funniest story about Ellen Sue and lemon cookies with too much powdered sugar," Michelle said. "I think she earned that tea set."

He remembered the story, pretty much a family legend. "Every time mom tells that story she claims to have coughed for a little bit longer on that powdered sugar."

"A parlor version of the fisherman's tale?"

"Accurate assessment," he agreed. "Is the furniture in here worth anything?"

"Anything is worth it for the right collector," she replied. "There are people who deal in both the fabrics and the pieces themselves. I can put feelers out if you'd like to see which would bring the best return."

"Please do that." He studied the upholstery. "If anyone in the family wanted this they would've stepped up by now."

Her smile, soft and wistful left him wondering what memory she was reliving. "They fit so well right here it's hard for me to imagine them elsewhere." Her eyes cleared. "Might be best to photograph them before we move them out. Someone is more likely to fall in love with the whole set."

His great aunt had kept her house and some of the original fixtures in excellent condition. She had good help with the maintenance at the end, and her standards had been met. Ellen Sue might've leased the land, but she'd kept full control here at the house.

"Tell me what's next," he said as they finished the circuit of the first floor and returned to the kitchen.

She pressed her lips together. "Once the inventory is done, I'll give you a wholesale versus retail assessment. Then you can choose how to proceed. If you're in a hurry to clean things out, I'll connect you with an auction house to give you a fair price on the entire lot."

There it was, another little hitch in her voice. Because of the memories attached to the house and belongings or because of the break-in at the shop? Since when was he too much of a coward to ask a question?

"If you go with an auction house," she continued, interrupting his speculation, "Y-you need to make sure that you've gone through every piece and removed any personal items."

"People leave things behind?"

She nodded. "If they notice, it can get awkward."

He'd never considered that. He hadn't given the intricacies of her business much thought at all. In

Michelle he saw a beautiful, intelligent woman with shared interests outside of her extensive knowledge and passion for antiques. During his previous trips into town, they would usually see each other at some local sporting event or a community activity where she was often working right alongside his great aunt.

"Should we head upstairs?" He moved toward the hall. "Those four-posters must be worth something." If he could talk antiques, maybe she'd open up about whatever was bothering her.

"No, no. We don't have to go up," she said in a rush. "I've already taken a bunch of pictures during appraisals we did before Ellen Sue died. I can use those."

Was she resisting the bedrooms because she felt the low hum of attraction between them? Now that she was within reach he wanted nothing more than to kiss her again. Did he have a chance at rebuilding something he should have given a real chance? Nothing about the last year had felt quite right. Though they'd only spent a couple of hours together, something had clicked into place.

It wasn't a reaction he would take for granted. Since seeing his extended family growing with spouses and kids at Ellen Sue's memorial and watching the Guardian Agency team settle into relationships, he'd felt almost jealous.

In some vague place at the back of his mind, Swann figured he'd have a wife and a couple of kids eventually. An assumption of how life was supposed to go. Then he got busy with law school goals, recruited by one of the world's wealthiest and most eccentric men, and it just didn't work out. Yet.

And now he was standing here with Michelle and thinking about things she might not even be interested in. At all or with him. He could ask, and would eventually, but the worry in her eyes, the skittishness bothered him. "So if you've already been through the rooms upstairs, why is the full inventory report taking so much time?"

She blinked owlishly, her gaze sliding away. Recovering, she faced him, her shoulders squared up and her chin lifted as if she was braced for a fight. "Ellen Sue's estate isn't my only client. And it's not like I have full-time staff to run the store and manage the website orders."

She started for the den, then seemed to change her mind, heading out the back door and sinking into the swing there.

"I'm not trying to be a jerk," he said, trailing

after her. He propped a shoulder against the upright, growing more curious by the minute.

If she needed help with some problem, he had resources, would put all of them in play for her. She had no way to know that, since the Guardian Agency didn't advertise. "We've never been in a hurry considering the leases on the land," he said. "Personally, I've been trying to figure out the best use of this house for the community as a whole."

"It needs a family." Her wistful voice floated on the evening breeze. Belatedly, her gaze snapped to his. "I only meant… your aunt always said that."

"I know." Ellen Sue had been heartbroken about not being able to have children, but she'd made up for it by making the whole town her own.

"We really aren't in any hurry, he said again. "You don't have to rush to move the pieces you want. Whenever we sell, the farm leases will be honored so no one will just move in and change everything overnight."

The brackets pinching her mouth relaxed a little, but that only made him want to kiss her. "You act like you have an investment in more than the antiques" he observed, testing her reaction. "Are you involved with one of those leasing farmers now?"

"What? No. Are any of them even under sixty? Or single?"

Then what was on her mind? "Those parameters don't stop some people."

She arched an eyebrow. "Both would stop me."

"I'm glad to hear that." Did he have a chance at restarting things here, the right way?

She stared at him and he wondered what she was searching for. Did he measure up? Her tongue slid over her lower lip, capturing all of his attention.

"Are you involved with anyone?" His voice sounded as ragged as he felt. He was definitely invested in her answer. "Personally, I mean." It seemed even his heartbeat paused, waiting for her reply.

"I..." She blushed and sidled toward the house. "I should go." The color that had flooded her cheeks a moment ago drained away. "You've had a long day and probably have more work ahead of you. Sorry about the whole baseball bat deal."

"You didn't answer my question." He kept his hands in his pockets, striving for a nonchalance and patience he didn't feel.

"I'd rather not," she said.

"Why avoid it?" he pressed. "It's an easy one. You're either seeing someone or not."

She folded her arms over her chest and straight white teeth nipped into her lip. "Why do you think it's your business?"

She had to feel something. There was no way she could be immune or oblivious to the chemistry sizzling like heat lightning across a dark sky. He didn't care what had started it or how long it had been. He hadn't forgotten her and he wanted to reconnect, to explore what might be under the surface of a good friendship.

He closed the distance, his gaze on her face, reading every subtle nuance. She didn't run, didn't flinch as he leaned down, slowly, until at last his mouth touched hers. He felt the tremble, and the gasp, soft as a whisper as it roared through him.

"Nolan," she murmured against his lips. Her hands smoothed up and down his biceps, her fingertips digging in as she rose up for another kiss.

He plundered, drawing her close and rediscovering the taste of her. Need pumped through him as he cupped her head and took the kiss deeper still. How had he managed a year without her? This, her, felt more like a homecoming than turning onto the long drive that led up to the house.

He eased back before he did something even more reckless than last time. "Michelle, tell me you're not seeing anyone. Please."

Her lips teased his jaw. "I wouldn't kiss you if there was anyone else." Instead of moving closer, she nudged him away. "That doesn't mean I'm going to hang around for your amusement."

Even though he deserved the reminder, it stung. "I meant to call. Forgive me." She let him take her hand, trace her fingers. "I never meant to make you feel used. It was more than that. For me."

She laced her fingers through his, then drew back completely wrapping her arms around herself. "I'm not about to be petty and lie." Her smile didn't quite reach her big brown eyes. "I enjoyed that night." She huffed a small laugh. "A lot. But shouldn't we learn from the past rather than repeat it?" Taking a deep breath, her gaze drifted away from him. "I'll go. Let's have coffee or something while you're here."

Coffee? Hell no. He was stuck, at least for the moment, convicted by his own mistake and at a loss as how to change her mind. "There's plenty of room for you to stay here and it's already dark. I can keep my hands to myself. If that's what you want," he added.

"I think that's what we both *need*."

He'd take that as a sign of hope, though the answer was in direct contrast to what every cell in his body was demanding. "All right. Though I'm going on the record as disagreeing with your opinion." He put enough humor behind the words to put a sparkle in her eye.

As much as he enjoyed flirting and dating, bringing Michelle light and amusement filled him with a swelling sense of accomplishment. "You were right that I have work. Do you want tea in the front parlor first?"

"No."

He leaned back from the sharp answer. Her eyes flared with blatant fear. Cautious of spooking her further, he tucked his hands in his pockets. "Michelle, what's really going on?"

She shook her head, her lips a flat line of denial.

"Better to tell me." He sat down on the top step and patted it for her to join him. He was immensely relieved when she did. "You'd be surprised by the grim scenarios my imagination can spin up."

"It's not a big deal." She rubbed her palms across her jeans.

But it was. She'd attacked him when he walked into a house he owned. She'd hidden her car in the garage and she didn't want to be at the front of the house. "Someone is after you," he stated, adding it up. "You're not here for the inventory, you're hiding."

And he'd wrecked her plans. Well, he was here and she didn't need to deal with the trouble alone.

"No, no." Her hand hit his chest and he belatedly realized he was crowding her, trying to soothe and comfort. "Not exactly. No one is after *me*."

She was lying. He let it go, hoping his silence would draw out more information.

"I'm here because there is a ton of work to do. You know I've always loved this house, the peacefulness of the whole place."

He waited her out, wary of making a move that would scare her away.

"Fine. I've had some trouble," she said. "But it isn't a big deal. Just a seller's remorse thing. Based on the nagging calls someone in the family thinks I have some heirloom jewelry or something that was included in a shipment from an auction house in Oklahoma by accident."

"You wouldn't be hiding all the way out here from nagging calls. At Plum's they were talking about a break-in."

"This town," she said, charmed and exasperated. Her smile was marginally better than her last attempt. "Yes, that happened too. The persistence in this instance is frustrating," she said. "I've told them I don't have the piece. I always review the items when they arrive. But they don't seem to believe me."

"Need a lawyer? I know a guy," he said.

"Stop," she said, bumping her shoulder gently to his. "I don't need a lawyer."

"What about protection? I can hook you up with someone reliable and subtle to prevent another break-in."

"Not you."

He was qualified and willing, but he didn't see either fact working in his favor right this minute. "Not me." He faked a wince and patted his ribs. "You saw how I dropped when you attacked me with a baseball bat. Just know that if you're afraid of something or someone I can make it go away."

"I guess I don't understand what lawyers do."

"We're a complex breed," he joked. "Let's just say my firm is multifaceted."

She relaxed, softening against him. "Thanks for the offer, Nolan. The LPD is aware of the situation and they're keeping an eye out."

He struggled against the idea that she was in enough trouble to need the police, but not him. Not that she knew anything about the true nature of his law practice in Chicago. But it did give him an idea for his next meeting with Brady. If the kid was as good as their client claimed, he could surely dig up something on the sellers behind Michelle's recent acquisition. A well-placed call or letter covered in legalese could clear this right up. He didn't want her to live in fear.

"Good. If whatever is going on has you rattled enough to keep baseball bats handy, stay here tonight." He stood and helped her up, then held the door for her. "If you leave, I'm only going to follow you to make sure you get home safely."

And he was likely to sleep in his car to keep an eye on her.

She scooped her hands through her hair, piling it high and letting it fall. He was taken back to that night and the feel of that heavy, dark silk brushing all over his skin.

"All right. I'll stay. Thanks, Nolan."

He had to be patient and earn back her trust

until she felt comfortable giving him the whole story. "Now that it's settled, I'm going to go get a little work done. Is it okay if I set up in the dining room?" The dining room also had a window facing the driveway, allowing him to be a buffer if someone did come around.

"It's your house," she said. "I only wish I could put in an offer."

"Speaking for the family, we'd love to sell to you," he said. He could see her here, updating the rooms with her own style while maintaining the charm and history Ellen Sue had created. "And in your case, we know the leases wouldn't be a problem. Unless you're wanting to get into farming yourself."

"No." She tilted her head. "Raising goats could work. It's lucrative." She laughed when he shot her a startled look. "I'm teasing, although goats would mow down the parlor upholstery in a heartbeat."

"That would be a crime," he said.

"Would it really?"

Amused, he set up his computer in the dining room while she retreated to the den. He was surprised how quickly a few hours had passed in that companionable quiet. Gamble expected him to focus all his attention on Connor Brady, but he'd gone digging into Michelle's situation, using tricks he picked up from Claudia. With a better timeline, he could test Brady's skill and know if the kid was as good as claimed.

And if he found something worrying? Well, he could get creative. They did it all the time with agency cases. If she was facing a real threat, he couldn't just wait around waiting for her to come to him.

CHAPTER 5

THE NEXT MORNING, Michelle wasn't convinced that sleeping with Nolan in the house was any better than staying out here alone would've been. She'd been restless all night, so aware of him despite being on opposite sides of the hallway with a stairwell and a bathroom in between the bedrooms.

Ellen Sue had thoughtfully decorated each bedroom as if she entertained on a weekly basis. If the house had been a little closer to town it would've made a wonderful bed and breakfast. This far out it was hard to imagine that kind of venture succeeding. Leavenworth wasn't exactly a hotspot for tourism. The visitors who did come through stayed in town if they spent the night at all.

She left the bed and tiptoed down the hallway to the bathroom, well-aware that a self-proclaimed light sleeper might hear every step. Nolan had stayed in the master, updated years ago with an ensuite bathroom for Ellen Sue's convenience.

Michelle didn't linger in the shower, just in case Nolan had forgotten how small the water heater was out here. Something a new owner would probably update right away. Along with the kitchen. Making something lovely out of this house and the surrounding land had always been a fun diversion when she visited Ellen Sue. Nolan's great aunt had been convinced the house was begging for new life. A new family, as she'd said last night.

Her hand involuntarily slid over her belly as she dressed for the day. Her body hadn't changed on the outside with the pregnancy and miscarriage, but there were times when she felt so hollow. Would she ever know what being a mother felt like?

She was halfway down the stairs when she heard Nolan's deep voice in the kitchen. He was on the phone, she realized. The conversation didn't sound like an outright argument, but it didn't sound all that friendly.

If not for needing coffee so badly she would have avoided the room, giving him some privacy. Then she saw him from the doorway, and lost all power of speech and thought. He wore only low-slung jeans and work boots. Apparently he'd used the shirt wedged into a back pocket as a towel.

Good grief, was it that hot outside already? It felt hotter than the sun in here. She hadn't heard him doing any work around the house, though she knew there were several things on the running list his mother kept up with.

Scooting around him, she flashed him a smile as she poured a mug of coffee. Carrying it out to the porch, she wandered away from the kitchen and the man who made her too aware of every secret fantasy she kept locked behind the wall surrounding her heart.

Except when it came to Nolan, that wall was nothing more than a wispy fog bank. It would be so nice to fall into his arms and forget that they lived in two different worlds.

She stared out at the tractor in the field, smiling with memories of Ellen Sue trying to do it justice during her painting phase a few years back.

REGAN BLACK

That woman wouldn't be cowed by a little harassment. Michelle needed to get herself back to work and the sooner the better, before Nolan got dragged into her mess.

The screen door at the kitchen squeaked and slapped closed, followed by the sound of boots on the porch. He came around the corner with a smile on his face. She almost complained that he'd put on a clean shirt.

"Good morning," he said, stopping just out of her reach.

"Morning." She raised her coffee cup. He had to know what he was doing, forcing her to make the next move. Oh, she wanted to move all right. But would a fling with Nolan Swann break her or give her closure? "Everything okay?"

He nodded and then gulped down coffee. "I hauled materials and tools from the barn already. I'd like to get the stairs on the other side of the porch repaired before it gets too hot."

Too late for her. "I'll paint once you're done," she offered. "There's plenty of leftover paint in the barn."

The wraparound porch had wide steps at the front and back doors, as well as a third stack that led down to the garden path between the house

70

and barn-turned-garage. Over the winter an ice storm had brought down a heavy limb, taking out the steps connecting the porch to the path.

"You mean it?" He arched an eyebrow. "That would help a bunch."

She smiled, pleased to be useful.

"I have a meeting up at the military prison this afternoon," he said. "And more calls and paperwork. Are you working here or at the store?"

She did a slow turn. "It's the storage unit for me today. Crystal will handle things at the store. With any luck, Officer Quinn will have some information on the person who broke in."

"Either way, the whole town is on alert for you."

He wasn't wrong. "I'm trying to be grateful," she admitted. "You know I don't want to be a problem."

"*You* are never a problem, Michelle." He reached out and tucked her hair behind her ear. "I'd best get to it."

"Right." She raised her coffee cup to her lips before she moved in for a kiss. "I can make breakfast."

"I won't turn that down."

She didn't mind the division of labor, enjoying

the delectable view of his working while she prepared a breakfast skillet with layers of shredded potatoes, sausage and eggs. His shirt was off again before long and she sighed. His jeans rode low on his lean hips and his muscles bunched and flexed as he knocked out broken treads. Her body remembered all of that strength poised over her in bed, the gentleness in those hands.

They'd been so good together that night. And careful too, yet she still turned up pregnant. For a few weeks anyway.

An irritated oath broke through the haze of memories. She gave the skillet another stir, ready to add the eggs, when he came in, sucking on the side of his hand. Spotting the blood trickling down his arm, she turned off the burner and followed him into the mudroom.

It was hard to regret the decision, crowding into the small space with the man of her dreams. His skin radiated warmth and the scent of sunshine as he washed his hand in the big sink.

"How bad is it?" she asked, ignoring the faint odor of copper in the air from his blood. "A scratch," he said.

"Let me see." They were hip to hip as she pulled his hand away from the flow of water. It kept bleeding. "Deep enough. When was your last tetanus shot?"

"Two years ago," he said. "Maybe three. Not more than that."

"Good." She opened the cabinet over the washer and dryer and pulled down the first aid kit mounted to the door along with a towel. Folding the towel into fourths, she pressed it gently over the wound, raising his arm over his head, above his heart.

With him leaning against the sink, they were close enough to kiss. Then again, his chest, lightly furred with golden hair, was within easy reach as well. "What happened?" Her voice cracked on the query.

He grinned, clearly aware of his effect on her. "Didn't see the nail when I reached to move one of the old treads."

"Mm." She gave his hand one more squeeze and then drew it back down between them, to apply the antiseptic and a bandage.

"You could kiss it and make it better," he suggested.

His voice was smooth as caramel. It was exactly what she wanted to do. All she could think about. She leaned down and touched her mouth to the base of his little finger. The contact should've been innocent, but it was dizzying.

Maybe she swayed, because suddenly his hands were on her hips, drawing her into his body. *Oh, my.* That glorious, confident touch seared her. No, she hadn't been inflating the experience. He was exactly as wonderful as she remembered. She wanted to feel all of him again and get lost in the way he satisfied her every desire.

But it didn't seem right to hop back into bed with him before she told him the whole story. "We should talk," she said, easing back.

"Later," he said on a growl, pulling her up to her toes for a kiss. She had to rest against the solid wall of his chest while his big palms caressed her spine and down over her butt. She felt off-kilter, yet protected. On the verge of a great adventure that was sure to have a happy ending.

The kiss spun out until she hoped it never had to end.

"God, I've missed you, Michelle," he said against her ear. The man had a way of making her feel special.

"Me too." She touched her lips to his chest, right over his heart. "I know this sounds needy, but while you're here I wouldn't mind picking up where we left off. If you're amenable."

She wanted to make new sexy memories with Nolan that she could enjoy even if they couldn't have a forever. They were here, together, and she was determined to savor the time they had right now.

"I'm amenable." He flexed his hips, letting her feel his arousal. "But I want to do things right this time. Let me take you to dinner tonight."

She wasn't exactly comfortable going out while someone was pestering her. "I can cook."

His lips tilted into the sexiest smile she'd seen on his face so far. "Breakfast does smell amazing. Think about dinner out." He brushed her nose with his. "I want to spoil you."

Dazzled by him, her system in a flutter from the kisses and those big hands, she agreed. What else could she do? Maybe over dinner she'd find a way to tell him what had happened. It probably didn't matter, it just felt wrong to share her body and keep that to herself.

He went up for a shower while she got breakfast back on track and he returned to the kitchen, just as she was serving up. In a dark button down shirt and slacks, he made her want to forget the food altogether.

He filled two mugs with coffee and carried them to the table. "I appreciate this." His stomach rumbled. "Thanks."

She loaded up a plate for him and gave herself a smaller serving. Either he was very hungry or running late the way he shoveled the food into his mouth. "Fabulous," he said, carrying his plate to the sink. "Next time, I'll handle the cleanup. The warden called and moved up my meeting." He bent down and kissed her cheek as if they did this every morning. "I'll catch up with you when I'm done."

He was gone in a few swift strides. Which was exactly how it should be, but *wow*. She needed to beware of this Nolan addiction.

It would be easy to get used to this, an ideal harmony between two people with excellent chemistry. Except he lived in Chicago and she had no idea what she'd do without her shop. Online business was growing, but she still had to be here in person to pack and ship the items sold.

Not today's problem, she thought driving over to the storage center, taking the direct route. She was more comfortable just knowing he was close. Nolan was amenable to a fling while they were both here. Something bigger than a one-night stand and less than wedded bliss.

She could find that happy medium with him. And she wouldn't just take, recent drama or not, she'd find a way to spoil him a bit too.

TODAY'S MEETING with the warden went better and Swann had gained permission to start working with Brady in a secure office. The online work would be monitored of course, but they weren't working anything confidential right now anyway.

Everything seemed brighter this morning and when he inadvertently bumped his hand on something, he smiled. Michelle's kisses were so sweet, so full of promise. He couldn't wait for dinner tonight. Couldn't wait for what he hoped followed when they got back to his great aunt's house.

After reading through the email update from Gamble, Swann felt outrageously confident about the meeting with Brady. The youthful prisoner wasn't nearly as excited to see him, but when he saw the laptop, he perked up.

Swann decided not to go straight at the issue of who framed Brady, or who he might willingly be covering for. Instead, he set the kid up with searches into Michelle's recent orders and her auction house contacts, just to see what he dug up while he sat across the room and made a few calls.

He knew Brady was listening as he spoke with Hank, taking down names of people they should interview or research for the case. Swann high-lighted names when they got a reaction out of the kid. He hoped Brady avoided poker games because otherwise the kid would lose his shirt.

A guard walked in about an hour before Swann was ready, stating that their time was up. He didn't fight it, just thanked the kid for his help and told him he'd be back tomorrow.

Outside in the rental car, he reviewed what the kid had found on auction houses in Oklahoma. Brady had created a spreadsheet with sale dates, buyers, and notations on high-value pieces. Swann hadn't asked for that, but it did help.

Leavenworth had several antiques dealers, each of them with a slightly different focus or style. Two had made purchases from the same auction house in the past year, but no one else had reported a break-in or attempted burglary.

He did his own search on the public police record and when he saw that Michelle had also reported a break-in at her house, and called for help when she'd been followed, his instincts went into overdrive. Now he understood why she'd retreated to Ellen Sue's place.

Uneasy, he called Claudia. "I'm sending you some information. I *think* a friend of mine is being targeted, but I don't know why." He gave her what he had. "Brady came up with the spreadsheet."

"It looks good." She was quiet for a minute. "He's really thorough."

"Good to know."

"You think he'll fit into the agency?"

"My gut says yes, if I can figure out how to get him out of here. Let me know what you find."

"Will do."

Swann ended the call and stowed his devices before heading to the LPD. Hopefully he could coax the full story out of Officer Quinn before coaxing Michelle out to dinner.

CHAPTER 6

THE NEXT MORNING, Michelle was still trying to remember the last time she'd had such a great time on a date. Nolan had taken her to Plum's since she wasn't up for anything fancier after a day mucking around in the storage unit.

As she'd promised Officer Quinn, she'd searched the recent shipment for any sign of items that shouldn't be there. It had been satisfying to report that she only had items she'd expected.

Over cheeseburgers and thick milkshakes, Nolan let her ramble about fulfilling online orders. It was fascinating to learn more of the details about his business in town helping his firm assess and investigate a possible wrongful conviction.

So normal and easy. When he went back to

Chicago, she knew it would be an uphill battle to find someone who matched up with her so well.

Returning to the house, Nolan had held her hand, as they'd walked along the porch talking about all the things Ellen Sue's house could be. He'd kissed her again and again and though she would've gladly fallen into bed with him, he slowed things down.

Her dreams had filled in the gaps until the next morning, over breakfast, she couldn't stop blushing about all the things they hadn't done. Yet.

Today, he followed her as she drove into town. She wanted to be open a full day, wanted to get back on track. He claimed he could handle his virtual meetings from her office. They parked in the lot behind the shop, but she wished she had a good reason to take him around to the front.

Instead, she had to walk him right through the remaining signs of the break-in and past the cluttered storeroom to her office. It would've been nice, at any point, to show him her best self.

"You have had some trouble," he observed, eyeing the repaired lock and the new security camera.

"Other than a broken glass-fronted bookshelf the damage was minimal."

"Not sure I'd call that lucky," he said. "Can I have a full tour?"

"Seriously?" She turned on the lights in the office and dropped off her purse and messenger bag. "I didn't think collections were your thing."

"Maybe I'm all about the tour guide," he said with a broad wink.

She couldn't hide her amusement and then found herself distracted by his hands and mouth as he blocked her exit. "This is not going to get the store open on time."

He backed away, putting his hands into his pockets. "Yes, ma'am."

She gave him a quick tour, pointing out her favorite acquisitions and a few pieces his great aunt would've loved.

"I can't claim to have the same passion as you and Ellen Sue, but I'm starting to see some appeal in the whole antiques thing."

"How so?"

"The history." He turned a slow circle. "You tell a story in every display. Where the piece is from, how it might've served a family and how it might enrich a new home."

She swallowed. "You've been thinking of family?"

"It's been on my mind," he said, smiling. The casual admission hit her hard. "I've seen a few friends settle down. Maybe the wife and kid vibe is contagious."

Her mind blanked. "Maybe," she echoed lamely. "I'll, um, have the doors open in about thirty minutes," she said. "I'm not expecting a crazy rush of customers, but we usually do brisk business from Thursday afternoons through the weekend."

"I'll be fine back here," he promised her, dropping one more kiss on her lips.

She checked the cash drawer and the receipts from yesterday and updated her financial register under the counter. When she was set, she unlocked the front doors. Following her routine, she grabbed the duster, also stashed under the counter, and started on the daily upkeep, adjusting displays as she moved through the store.

With Nolan in the back room, she struggled to concentrate. Her mind kept wandering over the next kiss and what might follow. They both wanted more and yet he was drawing out the inevitable and the anticipation was delicious.

Of course she still hadn't told him about the consequences of the last time they'd slept together. He wanted a wife and kids. He treated her with the affection and care he'd one day show his wife. She might as well be practice. He lived in Chicago. The doctors couldn't tell her for sure if she could have children.

This was worse than foolish to get so hung up on him. She should flip the sign in the door to 'closed' and march into the office. Tell him the truth. Let him walk away. But this was supposed to be a friendly fling. Did she want to wreck that too soon? She didn't understand what it was about Nolan that made her believe all her dreams could come true.

Continuing on her rounds with the duster, she made a mental list. His smile, good humor, and unshakable nature were at the top. He was definitely easy on the eyes and even better company.

Thankfully, the door opened and the bell overhead chimed, pulling her away from her ridiculous exercise. She smiled at an older woman and the younger, quite pregnant woman with her. Mother and daughter, she thought at once and another generation on the way. Michelle's stomach ached with loss.

"Good morning, ladies. Are you shopping for anything in particular?"

"The baby's room," the older woman said. "I

want to have tea parties with my granddaughter eventually, the way my grandmother did with me."

"It's tradition for each baby girl to get a tea set. Most of the time two, one to treasure and one to practice with," the mom-to-be explained.

"A lovely tradition," Michelle agreed. "Take your time. I have several on display and I recently acquired an extensive collection that isn't in the shop yet, but I'll have pictures up front when you're ready."

They meandered through the store and she enjoyed the soft hum of happy shoppers in the background as she organized an album of Ellen Sue's teapots and tea sets to share. Nolan emerged from the office and gave the women a friendly smile as he walked up to the counter.

"When you get a minute, will you take a walk with me?" he asked, low enough that the women wouldn't overhear and feel rushed.

She appreciated the thoughtfulness and agreed, wondering what he was after.

The bell over the door rang again and Nolan disappeared back to the office as another woman walked in. "Mrs. Marley, what a pleasure." She and Ellen Sue had been close friends for most of their lives, both of them devoted to the community.

The older woman beamed. "Michelle, they were talking at the salon about your window display. When did you get that desk in?"

"That one's fresh," Michelle replied, settling in. "You have a good eye." The woman loved to haggle and soon they were both grinning over the agreed upon price of the traditional secretary desk with original glass doors and flourishes on the skirting and claw feet.

With delivery arrangements made, Mrs. Marley walked out, thanking a gentleman who had held the door for her. Michelle prepared to check on the mother and daughter, but the gentleman walked inside.

"Quite a place."

"Thank you." At first glance, he didn't strike her as her normal clientele. Most of the men she worked with were older. She pegged this man closer to mid-forties, despite the receding hairline and weathered face and hands, his eyes were bright behind the silver-rimmed glasses and he appeared quite fit.

He asked smart questions and she warmed up to him, offering suggestions about matching furniture to a maple pineapple four-poster bed for a child's room. The pictures he showed her were exquisite.

"I came all this way because I heard such good things about your shop. I see now why you were so highly recommended."

The praise warmed her. "Thank you. I do love working with antiques and dealers and customers who appreciate the beauty and craftsmanship and heritage of these older pieces. It's a form of art to me."

"Do you ever do business with anyone outside of the state?"

"All the time," she said. "Traveling is more than half the fun, although I do participate in online sales as well."

"I agree about the travel. Always loved it." He pulled off his glasses, polishing them on a corner of his shirt while his gaze roamed around the store. "One of my favorite auction houses is down in Oklahoma."

A warning bell sounded in the back of her mind, and she tried to keep her cool. The comment didn't feel like coincidence after the upsetting messages and harassment of recent days. "There are reputable dealers all around the region. We're very fortunate."

"Mm-hm. So you vet everything?" He made a show of placing his glasses carefully on his nose as he looked around the store again. "How does that work?"

Her uneasiness grew exponentially. She shifted, putting herself between the mother and pregnant daughter in case this escalated. Was there a plausible, safe way to urge them out of the store? "Is there something in particular you're shopping for today?"

"Oh, yes."

He slipped his hands in his pockets which somehow made her more nervous. Was he carrying a weapon? "Can you show me to your smaller pieces? I'm looking for a necklace for my wife. Our anniversary is coming up."

She couldn't recall if he'd been wearing a wedding band, but the smaller items were up front in a case near the cash register. She guided him in that direction, away from the other customers. "I don't carry precious stones or high-value items, but I have a wide selection of vintage fashion pieces she might enjoy."

As she reached to open the case, he stuck the point of a knife into her belly, applying enough pressure to slice her shirt, but not her skin. The blade was cold.

"I can gut you like a fish," he said. "And I will. Be careful and cooperate."

"What do you want?"

"Hand over the necklace that was in the armoire. It's my property and I want it back. Today." The knife pricked her skin, a thin scratch. "Now."

"You're mistaken," she said. This must be the person who refused to believe her. She tried to scoot closer to the silent alarm under the register. "There was never any necklace in the armoire. The lot I received from Oklahoma didn't have anything other than what I purchased."

"Lying bitch." He shoved her forward and she caught herself on a console table.

The items displayed scattered and a sweet children's tea set tumbled to the floor in a crash of porcelain and fractured pale pink roses. Oh, she hoped that wasn't the one the mother and daughter wanted.

"Where is it? I put that necklace in the armoire myself and tracked it here. No one else has it, so here we are. Hand it over."

The convoluted logic was absurd, but she didn't

know how to point it out while she was on the wrong end of his knife. "I don't have a necklace worth all this effort."

He only shoved her again, this time toward the armoire. That took her further from the alarm and closer to innocent bystanders. "We'll look together."

She flinched away from that sharp point, searching for the first chance to put a piece of furniture between them. "I can't give you what I don't have."

"You have it!" he shouted.

That shout would draw attention. Nolan would charge in or one of the policemen on duty nearby. As long as the women didn't become hostages. "I don't."

"Stop lying! The armoire was gone when I came for it. The necklace wasn't in the house, either. I tracked the armoire to the auction house. The necklace wasn't there, hadn't been found or sold separately."

She pretended to stub her toe on the edge of a rug, pushing him away and ducking behind a four-foot tall bookcase. Nolan must have taken that walk. It was the only reason she could think of that he wasn't helping her.

"Nice move," he said with admiration. "Won't change a thing. I killed the auctioneer and the bitch who bought the lot from the family in the first place."

He'd just confessed to two murders. Bile rose in her throat. She wasn't feeling good about her odds, even with the bookcase as a shield.

"Now it's your turn to make a good choice." He waved the knife and sliced her sleeve. "Give me the necklace and I'll let you live."

He had her cornered. She cursed her miscalculation. She couldn't get to the register or the phone on the counter. Holding up her hands she promised to cooperate. "Search all you want. I've never seen a necklace worth killing over."

She hoped the mother and daughter had escaped. The back door hadn't chimed, but maybe they were hiding in the restroom. She didn't look around for fear of drawing the man's attention to them.

"Maybe my assistant found it," she improvised. "She would've called the jeweler or put it in the display next to the register."

"Show me."

He grabbed her as soon as she was within reach, putting that knife to her back and prodding her toward the front of the store. "Don't even try for the alarm," he said. "I know right where it is."

"Wouldn't dream of it," she snapped, angry now.

The way her window faced the street between the displays and the counter, no one would see anything problematic before it was too late. He'd thought this through. Forcing her against the wall, he tucked the knife away while he searched the display case and the boxes underneath.

She watched people walk up and down the sidewalk, oblivious to her problem. Then she saw Nolan, across the street, speaking with the mother and her pregnant daughter. "Those are primarily empty," she said, trying to get him out of here. If Nolan walked in, what would this bastard do?

Too late, he did just that, setting the bell tinkling over the door. The smile on his face faded to a perplexed frown. "You okay?"

"Maybe. Did you forget my coffee?"

"I picked up lemonade," he said with too much cheer.

If it was code, she didn't understand it. "I'd really like coffee. Can you go back, please?"

He grinned at her and then leaned over the counter. "Who's your friend?"

The thief jumped to his feet and pulled a gun, aiming it at Nolan.

Michelle didn't think, just shoved the thief over. It was enough for Nolan to grab him and drag him over the counter. She pressed the alarm while they wrestled. The gun fell away, but she couldn't get around them to grab it.

Instead, she picked up the folding stepstool and swung it at the thief's back. He staggered, found a chair and threw it at Nolan before he darted out the front of the store. Nolan followed him, but came back emptyhanded.

"Lost him." He turned the sign on the front door to 'closed' and turned the lock. "Police are on it." He came around and opened his arms. "Are you hurt?"

She shook her head and rushed into his embrace. "It's all better now."

"I've called in reinforcements," he said.

"More facets of law practice?"

Under her cheek, a low laugh rumbled through his chest. "You could say that."

He kissed the top of her head and she held on tight, reluctant to let him go even after the police arrived to write up the report.

Too shaky to drive, they left her car in town.

He held her hand throughout the trip back to the house, up the new porch steps and all way into the kitchen. "The women who were in shopping for a tea set want the unicorn teapot for sure. I showed them a picture."

"You're my hero, Nolan Swann." She kissed him, deeply, giving him all of the pent up emotion surging through her.

"Same goes, Michelle," he said against her lips. "You amaze me time and again." He tunneled his fingers through her hair.

She sighed against him and started unbuttoning his shirt, needing a new kind of comfort only he could provide.

He ripped the shirt away and she smoothed her hands over his chest. On an oath, he boosted her up and she wrapped her legs around his waist, her mouth molded to his until they were both breathless.

A sexy grin full of promises lit up his face and sent her pulse racing as he carried her straight up to the bedroom.

CHAPTER 7

NOLAN'S BODY was thoroughly satiated, but his mind wouldn't rest. With Michelle tucked up against him, sleeping soundly, her cheek pillowed on his arm, his brain turned over the solutions to this mess. He was positively livid the bastard had gotten away. The thief had nearly killed her. When he'd taken off her shirt, the sliced fabric and scratches enraged him.

He had tempered all of that in the moment, in the sheer enjoyment of being with her body and soul. But now, he couldn't shut it off.

Careful not to disturb her, he slipped out of the bed and retrieved his phone. He had text messages from Claudia, confirming the murders in Oklahoma. The last message asked who he wanted to call in for backup.

He had bodyguards on the agency payroll who could be here within hours. He also had resources and connections through Hank Patterson. After what had happened at the store and the incidents prior to Swann's arrival, it might be smart to call in everyone. He wasn't always a more-the-merrier kind of guy, but he refused to take any chances with Michelle. There was just too much at risk. Her life. His heart. Their future.

He asked for Colin, Hank and Swede, instructing Claudia to coordinate the response with the local authorities and let them know private bodyguards would be working this too.

He had to give the thief credit for being sneaky and playing dirty. The police had found a wig in a trash can around the corner and the glasses had been discarded a few yards away. He'd planned every detail. Claudia still didn't know the man's name or have a reliable description. Swann didn't care about names or anything else. The next time he had a shot, Swann would make the man suffer.

Michelle rolled over, her hand stroking the covers where he'd been. "Come back to bed," she said, her voice rough with sleep.

Her body was glorious in the spill of moonlight through the window. "You sure you don't want to see a doctor?"

"Not right now." She propped herself up on an elbow. "I should ask you the same question. You were the brawler."

"I'm good." He had tried to sort out when she started to matter so much, but when wasn't important. She was special to him. Priceless. Whatever sacrifice or adjustment he had to make to stay in her life, assuming she wanted him, would be an honor.

"We make a good team," he began.

"You were so cool with that lemonade line." Her smile was pure temptation.

He leaned down and kissed her and then slid between the sheets, cuddling her close. "I know I said I'd only stay for a few days, that we'd put the house on the market, but I'm not leaving until we have this guy under control."

She chewed on her lip. "You can't stay indefinitely. You have a career and a life."

"I'm a partner in a law firm with exclusive clientele. My job and practice is safe, trust me. I'll stay as long as you need me," he said. "As long as you'll have me."

He rubbed her palm with his thumb and stroked her back while her fingertips swept back and forth along his jaw. Something just tumbled into place deep inside and everything felt right. Clear. He was hers and he reveled in the sweet, lasting finality of it.

God help him if she didn't feel the same way. He'd give her time to come around. He wouldn't rush her or pressure her, but he wouldn't give her any reason or room to doubt his intentions.

With her curves pressed up against him, he tipped up her chin and kissed her. The feel of her hand in his hair, the soft catch in her breathing spurred him on. He wanted to give her so much pleasure she would never remember this day as anything but beautiful and perfect. The thief and those terrifying moments at the shop would be shoved away, relegated to a corner of her mind she rarely visited.

If that's all she took, if she never wanted to share a life with him, he could be content with that much as long as she was safe and happy. Finally, he slept until his phone rang again. Seeing Hank's number, he scrambled out of bed to keep from waking Michelle.

"You doing all right?" Hank asked.

Swann stepped into the bedroom across the hall. "We're safe for the moment. Did you get the update from Claudia?"

"We did. Swede and I are only a few hours out."

"Thanks," Swann said. "I can't cover everything out here without help. The cops are good people, but there aren't a lot of them and this guy plays dirty."

"That's what teamwork is about, my friend," Hank assured him. "We've got your back."

Swann ended the call and returned to the bedroom to find Michelle sitting up this time. "I'd really like to wake up beside you."

"Really?"

"It is one thing we haven't done," she said with a pointed expression. "Is there more trouble?"

"No." He kissed her. "That was the backup band," he quipped. "They'll be in town by breakfast."

"What did you do?" She queried without moving from her spot on the bed.

All he wanted was to crawl back into bed and forget the rest of the world existed, but that would be suicide. "The thief who attacked your shop won't quit. He's out there somewhere making a plan and he's demonstrated the skill to follow through. As much as I would like to be all you need, I can't handle this alone."

"I'm not going to let you fight the battle by yourself, with or without the backup," she said. "I'm done hiding out. The man was after a necklace, with my connections maybe I can help narrow that down."

"Baby, I understand. I don't want that for you either. We have to be smart here, and we have to stay safe. That means bringing in some help. One of my bodyguards and a couple other people, former Navy SEALS. The three of them have experience with investigations, manhunts, you name it. They'll work with the authorities and we'll drop a net over this guy."

"So you won't send me away?" she asked.

"Never." He touched his forehead to hers. "I just want you safe. We'll get through it," he said. And if something went wrong? Tomorrow wasn't guaranteed. If he didn't have the guts to tell the woman he loved his feelings now, when would he?

"When we catch this murderous thief I'd like to take more time with you, time without chaos or trouble. I'm not walking out of here and never calling again."

Her slender hand curled around his fingers,

and she lifted his hand to kiss his palm. "I really should have called you," she said. "We had no expectations about that night, but afterward. I missed..." Her voice trailed off.

"I missed you too," he said softly. "Far more than I expected. That night never felt like a one-night stand to me, no matter what we said going in. Being back, I know without a doubt that this is what I want, Michelle. You and me, sharing a home and a life. I'd love to fill this house with kids and let them run wild. I want to know that when you go to an auction, you'll be coming home happy, delighted with a new find, eager about cleaning it up for the shop."

He couldn't stem the tide of words, even when the color drained from her face.

"I'm pressing, I'm sorry. Tell me to shut up." A tear glistened on her lashes. "I don't want to wait, but it's too much too soon."

"Nolan, don't wait. Just say what's on your mind."

SHE WAITED, frightened and excited about what he might say.

"It's on my heart really," he said. "I love you, Michelle."

Oh, how she loved him right back. And how selfish of her to want to just revel in it, to let him believe in that future full of kids when she didn't know if she could have any. After losing his baby. Was anything more screwed up than the way she was about to wreck this moment?

"Nolan—"

"You don't have to give me an answer, not while things are crazy. Just know that I love you, without strings or reservations or any conditions. We can work out the rest when this is over. Yes, I have a vision of how I want it to go, but more than anything I want you to be happy, to have everything you dream of, even if it's not me."

"Stop." She pressed a finger to his lips. "Thank you for all of those assurances. Whatever happens, hear this. I love you too."

He would walk away as soon as he knew the truth and the broken part of her heart believed he should. The pain of that moment had already set in, even as she clutched his hand.

"I'm not going to let anything happen to you," he vowed.

"That's not what this is about," she said.

Climbing out of bed she started to dress. She couldn't tell him now, not when he needed to focus on capturing the thief. "Tell me what you need me to do today. "I'm certainly not going to just sit in a corner and watch."

"I expect him to make another run at you. I'll discuss it with the others, but the best bet is to keep an eye on the places he knows. Your store, your house, and the storage center. Once we have those bases covered, we can make a plan to draw him out and deal with him on our terms."

She was so thankful, so happy to know she wasn't alone in this battle. She couldn't see a way that she would have survived any of this if he hadn't been here. But what she felt was more than obligation or even gratitude. She had fallen in love with this man, probably that first day up on the roof and it had just grown little by little with every subsequent meeting. There was a depth to their connection that went deeper than anything she'd known before.

Aside from the one secret she couldn't seem to speak out loud, she wanted to share everything with him. "Any chance you need weapons for this take down?"

"What are you talking about?"

"Ellen Sue began collecting guns a few years ago."

He gaped at her. "You're kidding."

"Not a bit. I had a line on a set of dueling pistols and she got excited about it. She always had the shotgun, as you know. But she added revolvers to her collection and some really unique guns. All in working condition. She kept them in the basement," Michelle finished.

"Let me guess, you'd go out for target practice and then come back to the parlor for lemon bars and tea."

"Pretty much," Michelle admitted. The amusement in his eyes was worth it.

"All that firepower and you came at me with a baseball bat."

"Lucky for you," she teased. She crawled across the bed to kiss him. "Let's grab a shower and make breakfast together."

"Another fantasy of yours?" he asked.

She nodded. "Goes along with waking up beside you."

She would have spent every ounce of hot water with him in the shower, given a choice. But there were things to do and so much to enjoy as she watched him put a plan into motion.

Phone calls to the sheriff's office. Conversations between him and men she had never met. He didn't close her out of any of it, but he didn't exactly invite her opinion. There weren't any introductions, no opportunities to define her role in this beyond the fact that she had purchased a lot at auction and drawn the ire of a deadly thief.

Someone named Claudia called, sounding grim as her voice filled the kitchen. "I still don't have a description. I'm getting worried."

"Now you know how I feel when you guys go off the radar," Nolan replied.

"Yeah well don't do that either," Claudia scolded. "I think your best bet is to use the necklace as leverage."

"You mean the necklace we haven't found and know nothing about?" Nolan asked.

"The armoire where he said he stashed it is empty," Michelle said. "I've searched the storage unit and the shop from showroom to the back door. No necklace."

"Which means we have to convince him the necklace is somewhere else," Nolan said. "I can work with that."

Her skin warmed and her heart pounded at the expression on his face. It was a lovely thing to be treasured, she just wish she felt worthy of it. Almost worthy wasn't the solid foundation to build a relationship on.

"That guy you've been interviewing has the skills to help," Claudia said. "The initial research was impressive. Why not have him plant a few news reports to drive your thief in the right direction."

Nolan pushed a hand through his hair. Another trip to the prison meant leaving Michelle in someone else's care. "Why is it you can't plant things in this situation?"

"Let's call it orientation." Even Michelle heard the smile in her voice. "Besides, it'll give you something *productive* to do while you're waiting for the cavalry to arrive."

Nolan paced the porch, thinking through her suggestion. "Guess we'd better head back to the prison," he decided. "At least I know you'll be safe there while I try to get another meeting with the guy I want to bring on board."

"You're not leaving me behind?"

"Absolutely not."

They sealed it with a kiss and headed out.

CHAPTER 8

ON THE DRIVE to the prison, Swann checked in with everyone. The officers watching her shop reported nothing unusual. Colin, Hank and Swede had split up to cover her neighborhood and the historic district, but so far there were no signs of the thief.

The quiet worried him more than an attack would have done. He hoped like hell that his plan forced the thief into action.

Though he'd wanted Michelle to stay with a deputy sheriff at his great aunt's place, she would've rejected the idea. He didn't want her out of his sight either. She was still holding something back, but unless it was a declaration that she didn't want to be with him, he didn't care. After last night, he was confident they could work though any other issues as long as they were together.

Arriving at the prison, she had to wait up front for security reasons while he spoke with the warden. Once again, he spun a tale of how he needed Brady's expertise as a consultant while the motions Gamble filed worked through the system. Having been the scapegoat, it would take time to prove Brady's innocence.

At last he convinced the warden to let him meet with Brady in a private conference room with a laptop hardwired to the internet.

"In the case I'm working, the thief is after a valuable necklace," Swann began. "I need you to fabricate a story that shows this list of high-ticket items has been moved from Leavenworth to Kansas City for appraisal. I have descriptions for you to use." It was all guess work, but what else did they have?

"You want me to plant fake news?" Brady confirmed.

"Yes, please. The sooner, the better."

"Another test?" Brady scowled at the laptop.

"As far as I'm concerned, you've got the job, kid. It's a matter of where you do it. And whether or not we can pay you," he added. "For a while yet you might have to do it here, but we are working every angle to get you out. Easier if we could give the real culprit to the court."

"I don't know." Brady shook his head. "If I recant—"

"Tell the truth," Swann interrupted.

Brady glared. "It could get ugly for the others still in that unit."

"Not if they're innocent."

Brady scrubbed at his face. "That's some clean, black and white theory you're spouting, but it isn't reality."

"Okay, so a few eggs get cracked. On the other hand, national security gets breached for real next time." He had the kid ready to talk, he could see it in his eyes. "Wouldn't it be better if the person who *did* the crime did the time?" Swann pressed.

"Generally speaking I agree," Brady admitted, his gaze dropping to the floor.

"From what I can piece together whoever put that information at risk and blamed you could very well get away with it again and blame someone else."

"Damn it. I've worried about that." He sighed. "I would like it if my mom could be proud of me again."

"Give me a name."

Brady gave him the name and more, explaining in a rush that he didn't willingly cover for a commanding officer, but he hadn't protested the charges when the CO promised not to implicate a female soldier in the unit. He even walked Swann through the methods the CO used to make sure Brady took the fall.

Swann was about to give the kid some encouragement that the law firm could help him clear his name when an alarm sounded through the prison. "What the hell is that?" he asked.

"Not internal. Something must've happened outside," Brady replied. "Do I stop or keep going?"

"Keep going." Swann said. "I'll clear it with the warden. Give me a minute."

Swann stepped out into the hallway and saw a cluster of guards near the visitor's desk. Exactly where he'd left Michelle. Cursing himself for a fool, he rushed over. "What's the trouble?"

"Possible kidnapping," one guard said.

"Possible?" Swann echoed. How could they not *know*?

"Another visitor walked in, registered at the desk and then spoke to the pretty brunette lady sitting over there. I couldn't hear what they said."

Swann managed not to roll his eyes. This was a military prison, supposedly wired for audio and video to cover every security consideration. "Did the woman leave willingly?"

The guard from the desk piped up, "Looked like it from my angle, but I don't think she was happy to see him."

"Where's the name, the ID he showed you?" Swann demanded.

"I-I'm not sure that's allowed," the guard stammered.

"Forget it." He had a more reliable resource a few yards away. He charged back toward the room they'd loaned him for Brady. "Give me anything you can from the prison surveillance feeds."

"Seriously?"

Swann nodded once. "Do it. Now."

Swann's stomach twisted into knots while he waited for any information. How had this even happened? She should have been safe right here in a prison for the single hour he needed to get a handle on the man who'd attacked her at the store. Where had he miscalculated?

He was sending crazed texts to Hank, Swede and Colin, putting them on alert to the new crisis when Brady finally said, "Sent the surveillance feeds to your phone, sir."

Swann stared at his phone, watching a man march Michelle out of the prison. He couldn't see a weapon, but there was no other reason the woman he was in love with would walk away. "Call me Swann."

Brady cocked his head. "I'll try."

How had it come down to this? He'd done everything right and still failed her. He would have to berate himself more thoroughly later. Right now he had to find a way to save her.

His phone rang in his hand and he answered. "Colin, tell me you have something."

"They're headed back toward Leavenworth," Colin reported. "Want me to intervene?"

"No, just keep following them so we know where they are. I'll tell Hank and Swede and move them into place to cut him off. Call you back when we have a plan."

"Mr. Swann?" Brady said. "I've notified the sheriff. And, I, ah..."

"Say it," Swann ordered. "Everything you do is on my head."

Brady's eyebrows arched. "Well, I'm looking at

the security feeds around Ms. Korbel's store and her storage unit."

He didn't recall giving Brady that information, but that's exactly the kind of initiative that would help him fit in at the Guardian Agency. "And?"

"The man who escorted her—"

"Kidnapped her," Swann corrected.

"Right." Brady swallowed. "He's been watching the antique store and the storage unit too. And her house."

Swann swore. "Find out everything you can."

"Yes, sir."

Swann's mind was racing when he recalled something his protectors and even Claudia said on occasion. Sometimes the simple solution was the best one. He dialed Michelle's cell phone. It rang once, then twice.

"Nolan, let me handle this," she said in a rush.

He heard a deeper voice in the background give a command.

"You're on speaker now," she said.

"Call off your dogs," a deeper voice ordered. "I spotted the one tailing us and I know the cops are keeping tabs on her."

"Of course they are," Swann countered. "You've

caused too much trouble. Let her go and I'll tell them to let you pass on through town."

"Call them off," the man shouted. "Or there's no guarantee she lives."

"Pull over and let her out of the car. She'll give you her keys or codes and you can search for whatever you need," Swann said, trying to negotiate.

"If it was that damn easy, I'd have my property already. She's hidden it and I want it back today."

"I don't have the diamond necklace you described," Michelle said. "I've never set eyes on anything so extravagant or elaborate at an auction. Heirloom jewelry isn't my specialty."

She was feeding them details and he glanced at Brady to see the prisoner was picking up on the clues, brow furrowed and gaze intent as his fingers flew over the keyboard.

"Let her go," Swann said again. "You're making a huge mistake."

"The mistake is thinking you can keep my property," the man said.

Brady waved, catching Swann's attention. He hurried around the desk to read the information on the monitor. Lowry Gould was listed as released on parole after an abbreviated prison sentence for aggravated assault during a string of burglaries in a wealthy Dallas neighborhood. Gould had been caught in Oklahoma after shoplifting and stealing gas from a convenience store on his escape route. Several items listed as stolen had been found, but an heirloom diamond necklace valued at over two million dollars was still missing.

The pictures of the piece resting on sapphire blue velvet and later around the throat of an A-list celebrity on the red carpet were astonishing. If Michelle had found *that* in the lot from the Oklahoma auction house she would've notified the authorities immediately.

"Lowry Gould? This isn't the way to keep your ass out of jail."

"I'm not going back," Gould said, his voice cold. "No one gets hurt if this bitch gives me my property and you stand down. Starting with this guy on my tail. Call him off."

"I don't know what you're talking about," Swann said. "How the hell would I know where you are?"

There was a muted conversation on the other end of the call and Swann exchanged a look with

Brady, who shrugged. Neither of them could make out the conversation.

"Nolan?"

His heart seized. "Michelle. Talk to me."

"He's holding a gun on me," she said with profound calm. "I'd appreciate it if you would let me handle this. Once he sees I don't have his necklace—"

Gould started shouting obscenities. Swann ground his teeth, his temper rising.

"Once he sees I do *not* have the necklace," she started over. "I'm sure he will let me go."

Swann, looking at the thief's history, didn't believe that for a minute. Michelle had to be aware of the danger she was in. "Do you trust me?" he asked.

The line went dead before she could answer. Swann swore. "See what you can find on Gould, the robberies, or anything else," he said to Brady. "Forward whatever you have to my cell phone."

"Sure thing," Brady replied, fingers flying over the keyboard.

Two texts, one from Colin and one from Hank had come through during the brief call.

He ordered Colin to stop tailing the thief, giving him directions for an alternate route to the storage unit. He'd asked for Michelle's trust and he had to trust her in turn. The storage unit was more isolated and odds were high she would guide the thief there, rather than risk any bystanders in town coming to harm.

The necklace was *not* in the store. Michelle had searched on her own, and the police had gone through everything after yesterday's attack. Nothing remotely resembling that necklace was there.

Notifying the LPD, the authorities agreed to stay on the shop in town while the others coordinated a stealthy approach to confront Gould at the storage unit.

MICHELLE HAD no idea how she was going to get out of this. She trusted Nolan, but how would he know what to do and when? Surely he'd call the police for help rather than come alone.

"I really don't have your necklace," she said as the car rolled to a stop at the storage center security gate.

"I don't believe you," the thief replied. "Give me your code."

She hesitated, caving in a hurry when he pressed the gun to the top of her thigh. Although she hadn't provided any direction, he drove straight to the building for her unit. "How long have you been watching me?"

"Long enough to know you have my property."

What would he do when he realized she'd been telling the truth all along?

She hoped Nolan figured out she was leading the thief to the storage unit. She couldn't bear the idea that someone in town might get hurt because of one man's obsession. Bad enough that Nolan was undoubtedly on his way. He only looked like a city-boy afraid to get his hands dirty. He'd been raised in this area and he knew how to get things done.

"You really don't have to do this. Not this way," she said.

"I want what's mine," he replied. "Hand it over and this whole mess is done."

She couldn't afford to take him at his word. "You broke into my house and shop. You know I don't have that necklace."

"Quit bitching. You're still alive."

But for how long?

"Move!" He ordered. "I've waited too long to

leave empty-handed." The thief hauled her out of the car and shoved her inside the building. The air, cool and dry, washed over her. Too bad it couldn't wash away the fear. He dogged her, nearly stepping on her heels all the way to her storage unit. Though her hands shook, she got the key into the lock and the door open.

"Hit the light," he ordered.

She obeyed, already dreading the destruction as he started searching. She didn't keep many pieces of heirloom jewelry. Nothing of significant value. Her clientele didn't run to that market. If the police and sheriff's departments were keeping tabs as promised, they would know from her code and the security camera that she had come through the storage center gate. How long would it take them to arrive?

"If I had found something significant," she began, "I would have spoken with the auction house or reached out to a jeweler who specialized in heirloom pieces."

"Not this," he said. "You've kept it. Only a fool would give it away."

As he continued deeper into the unit, she crept closer to the open door. Consumed with his search, he didn't realize he'd left her an escape. Her storage unit was organized in 3 aisles, one on each wall and a shelving unit that ran the length of the space down the middle. When the thief turned at the end, Michelle bolted for the door.

She made it to the hallway, stretching up to pull down the rolling door on her way through the opening. Two gunshots sounded and she gave a small scream, as the bullets hit the door instead of her. The sound reverberated all around her and she had no idea how smart it was to stand here and hold a door closed against an armed man. More bullets crashed into the metal door and then he was fighting to open it again. She held the door down, putting all her weight behind it and prayed somebody would get here in time to help. Her head start was gone. And as she looked up and down the aisles she knew if she let him out, her odds diminished. She fought to get the door closed all the way so she could throw the latch. Even that might buy her enough time to get out.

Where were the police or the sheriff? Or anyone else for that matter? She really thought Nolan knew her well enough to figure out where she'd gone, where she had led the thief. The storage unit was the only place she could think of that would keep him busy until law enforcement could show up.

The thief was stronger than her, and the door jumped up a few inches as they fought for control. She gave a start when he yanked the door up and fired the gun simultaneously, the bullet barely missing her toes. The shock gave him an advantage. She had to relinquish the door and make a run for it.

Giving the door a shove with all her strength, Michelle ran. Her main concern was getting around the first corner without getting shot. She heard the rattle of the door rising but didn't dare look back. There was nowhere to hide, not in here. Unless she could get outside it was simply a matter of time before he found her inside the building.

She scrambled around the corner just ahead of another gunshot. The window in front of her shattered and the rain of glass falling on the cement floor was a strange bright twinkling counterpoint to the ragged pounding of her heart.

She took the last corner, the back door in sight, skidded to a stop, face to face with the thief. "Search the storage unit," she cried. "Toss everything until you're satisfied. Take what you want.

Just let me go, please." She had to get out of here before Nolan charged in.

His cold hard eyes, full of venom and bitterness, told her how this would end. She was cornered and out of options. The chime sounded as the front door of the building opened. The thief swore and lunged for her.

She tried to anticipate his attack, but she wasn't quick enough to evade his bruising grasp. "Get off me!" Twisting and thrashing only made it worse. She tried to kick at his legs but it was no use.

"Get me out of this or I kill your boyfriend." His voice was a menacing growl at her ear.

Boyfriend? Nolan was so much more than that. Unless he wasn't. Were they just hooking up for convenience? It hadn't felt that way to her, but… That was *not* the point just now, but her mind was determined to escape even if her body was stuck.

She wanted to survive, but more, she wanted Nolan to survive. The thief shoved the barrel of his gun into her ribs as Nolan came flying around the corner.

"Let her go," he demanded. "You might be after a necklace, but you've picked a hell of a fight. By touching her you signed your death warrant, Gould."

"Stay back, pretty boy," Gould snarled. He backed toward the door, dragging her with him.

"If you're lucky I'll leave her alive at the county line. Follow me and her blood is on your hands."

Nolan's blue eyes roved over her. "Are you hurt?"

"She will be," the thief said, yanking her hair so hard her eyes watered. The gun pressed deep under her ribs. "Either I walk or you plan her funeral."

"Nolan, please," she begged. "It's the only way."

CHAPTER 9

"THE HELL IT IS." Swann hoped the others were in position by now. He was going to dismantle this man one limb at a time for putting hands on Michelle. "Let her go."

"As soon as you hand over my property." Another step closer to the door. "That necklace is mine."

"Let her go and I'll put all my people on it," Swann said. "They can track it down with a little time."

"I'm out of time," Gould said. The gun still pressed to Michelle, he used her as a shield to get outside. "Still have plenty of leverage."

Swann followed as close as he dared, praying Colin, Hank and Swede were in position to cut off the thief's escape. Unless he had a second vehicle, he'd have to use Michelle to get around to the side of the building where he'd parked.

"Stay back, you son of a bitch!" Gould shouted.

What would it take to move that gun? "Can't blame me for making sure you'll keep your word." He had to hold the bastard's attention and separate the gun from Michelle.

Hands held out wide, Swann trailed after them. Somehow he would make this up to her. If she wouldn't let him stay and be part of her life, he would hire someone to be her permanent body-guard. He'd make sure this was the last time her career put her in danger.

But they had to get through this first.

Gould wasn't going to quit, whether or not Michelle had the necklace. Everything Brady and Claudia had found pointed to a vindictive, remorseless man capable of terrible violence since getting out of prison.

If Swann let Michelle go as a human shield now, she wouldn't survive and he'd never forgive himself. As long as Gould had a gun on her, no one could take an easy shot. Swann had to make the first move, create an opening.

And it had to be now.

Swann caught Michelle's gaze, willing her to understand that he wouldn't back down or let Gould hurt her. The man was trying to hurry her along and she was trying to slow him down without making it too obvious. Smart woman.

He had to move fast or the window of opportunity would be gone. None of the men backing him up would take a shot while she was in jeopardy. The three of them were out there, watching closely, ready to act. They were professionals, but for Swann this was personal.

"Tell me what you need," Swann pleaded with Gould. "I'll trade anything for her," he said. He stutter-stepped, as if he intended to close the gap.

"The only trade I'll make is for the necklace," Gould sneered.

He was lying. "Whatever happened to that thing, we had nothing to do with it," Swann insisted. "Let her go, man." This time he took a big step forward, hoping to draw Gould's focus. "We've never seen the piece you stole."

The bastard took the bait, leveling a gun at Swann for the second time in as many days.

Swann and Michelle acted at the same time. She drove her elbow into thief's gut and he rushed forward to tackle the thief.

Gould pulled the trigger, thanks to Michelle he missed, the bullet sailing high and wide as Swann took him to the ground. The thief's head bounced off the rough surface of the parking lot. Swan pummeled Gould's face, using his size to keep him down, knees clamped on the thief's ribcage. A law degree and a high-rent office in Chicago didn't mean he couldn't fight with his fists when it mattered.

Michelle mattered.

"Stop! Stop, Nolan!" Michelle's voice sounded far away. Gould was groaning, still conscious, still a threat. He kept at punching.

Colin was closer, and brave enough to take Swann's shoulder. "Enough, man. We're here. We've got it."

Swann let Colin haul him back once Hank and Swede closed in on either side of the thief.

"Go on, boss. Take a minute," Colin suggested, aiming him at Michelle.

She rushed straight into his arms and he held her close as Hank, Colin, and Swede dragged the thief away.

He held Michelle close to his chest, sheltering her from the thief's ugly protests as the police took Gould into custody. "You're okay?" he asked.

"Let me see your hands," she said.

"It's fine." He swiped the back of a hand across the hip of his jeans, far more concerned with getting her clear of this crisis than the stripe of blood he left behind on the denim. "You saw the other guy," he joked. "You were amazing." He pulled her in for another long hug. "We need to get you out of here."

"Let's lock up the storage unit first," she agreed. "I'll come back and straighten things out later."

"We will," he said without thinking, his pulse still kicking from the fear and the fight. She shot him an odd look, but slipped her hand into his, fueling his hope that they could sort out a future that worked for both of them.

When they came back outside, she looked around him, watching the paramedics tend to Gould. "What will happen to him?" she asked.

"Jail time for sure. With his record, five to ten years is a safe bet for the attempted burglaries alone. Once we tack on assault, deadly weapons—" He stopped himself as her big brown eyes rounded. "His fate is irrelevant. The police will sort it out."

He would've killed Gould with zero regrets given a chance. A smarter man would be a little scared about his disregard for that particular life, but the thief had crossed a line when he'd kidnapped and threatened Michelle. It made no difference that she'd handled herself in the crisis or that she was safe and whole now. He would see the man rot in jail for touching the woman he loved.

Loved. He was in love with Michelle. He'd already told her once and he wanted to tell her every day for the rest of his life. He treasured that reality, let it settle around his heart. If recent years with the Guardian Agency protectors had taught him anything, love could bridge tremendous challenges. It was as steady and affirming as the sun breaking through a bank of storm clouds. He wanted to tell her right now, eager to share his revelation. Then again, he wanted it to be private and special, not something he blurted out in front of witnesses, friends or not.

"Whatever happens in court," Swann vowed, "he won't get close to you or your shop ever again." He guided her around the emergency vehicles, wishing they could wait until tomorrow to give their statements. Instead, he settled for holding her hand through the questions.

He did avoid the media that had gathered just

beyond the police barricade. The greater community was *not* his concern right this minute. He wanted her out of here, tucked away somewhere safe so he could spoil her a bit. If he had any hope of figuring out their next step as a couple, he needed her to be confident that his feelings had nothing to do with the crisis. He didn't want to live another minute without her, even if that meant moving back to Leavenworth.

First, he needed to find his friends and after that he needed to speak with Brady and let him know he'd done well.

Colin stood by his car, catching up with Hank and Swede as if they'd bumped into each other at a bar, rather than wrangling a criminal. The bodyguard grinned when Swann and Michelle joined them. "Looking good, boss." Colin stretched out a hand. "Thanks for the invite."

Swann pulled Colin in for a one-armed hug, slapping his friend's shoulder. "Thank *you*." He tried to add more, but his throat closed up. He'd come too close to losing her. Stepping back and sliding his arm around Michelle's waist, he introduced her to the others, first names only and naming them as friends.

Michelle smiled, a little shy. He didn't miss the

wonder in her gaze as she tried to figure out how he knew these men. She thanked each of them in turn. It gave him time to regain his composure.

"Thank you all," he managed at last. "I don't know what I would have done without your help." He glanced down at her knowing all three of them understood the emotions rolling through him.

When they were allowed to leave he ushered her to his rental car, opening the passenger door for her. For a moment, he paused, indulging himself in another sweet kiss. She was alive. They'd made it. Now he just had to iron out the details.

He looked out toward the highway, all that flat ground had once felt like a trap. Now he saw it with fresh eyes, and as the prairie stretched out to the horizon he saw hope and a future he wasn't expecting, but he definitely wanted to claim.

Once they were on the road, he reached over and caught her hand, lifting it to his for a kiss. He took her hand in his, lifting it to his lips for a kiss. "How about some lemonade on the back porch to start?" he asked, giving her hand a squeeze. "There are some things I'd like to talk about."

MICHELLE'S NERVES WERE FRAZZLED, her thoughts a jumble of questions, what ifs, and impossible hopes that hovered just beyond her reach. Did he want to discuss the legalities of the house, or was there something more personal on his mind? She wasn't sure she could handle any more on either front. The words 'I love you' danced on the edge of her tongue, but he lived in Chicago, he wanted a family and she wasn't sure she could be what he needed.

She could be the friend and fling he wanted for right now, but long term? She wasn't sure she could be what he needed to make his own dreams come true, no matter how much she loved him.

"Nolan," she began. "You should know I never found the necklace the thief was after." He needed to know more than that, but it was a logical place to start.

"No worries. I imagine it was stolen somewhere long before the lot got to you. I have someone tracking it down as we speak."

She gave him a long look. How was it he looked even sexier with a few scrapes along his jaw and knuckles? "Do I want to know who?"

"Not right now." His smile, a little crooked due

to the swelling around his lip, let her know he would share the details in time.

She really shouldn't encourage that kind of lasting intimacy. They weren't on the same long-term path. "I know we thanked the others but I should thank *you*. The timing might have been a fluke, but..." She couldn't finish the thought, couldn't get out the words that she was in love with him.

They drove through town and he stopped to confer with the police officer guarding her shop. By the time he parked the car at the side of the house, her body was trembling with the adrenaline in her system.

"Aw, sweetheart," he said, noticing her reactions. "It's over now. Relax." He came around to her side of the car and opened her door. Helping her out, he pulled her close, his hands sifting through her hair and his lips soft. "It's over. You were so brave, but it's over. I've got you."

"I thought he would kill you," she stammered. "I-I didn't want that."

"My hero," he said with a smile. "I didn't want you to get hurt either." He lifted their joined hands out wide. "Look at us. We made it, together. In fact

I'd like to keep that going. The together part," he clarified.

Words that should've made her heart soar threatened to break it. "What are you saying?" she asked, cautious.

He guided her along the garden path to the house. "Well, I have to work out some details but I'd like to stay in Leavenworth. Ideally with you. Together. As in a couple." He touched her chin, held her gaze captive with his. "I love you, Michelle. It feels like I always have." He brought her hand to his chest, covering it with his own. "I love you. I'm done in Chicago if it means leaving you."

Heartache turned her knees to water and she leaned on him for support. Naturally, he caught her close, his big body strong and steady. She had to find a way to let him go. "I don't know that I want to live in Chicago," she began with a lie. If she had any confidence she could give him the family he desired, she'd follow him anywhere. Still, it was better than blurting out a truth that would hurt him.

"We could live here. Breathe new life into this big house," he said as they walked up the porch steps he'd repaired. "We can have over-sugared lemon bars in the parlor when guests drop in. I might even enjoy it, assuming you can tone down the upholstery."

He made her laugh and that was priceless. Oh, how she wanted to be part of the picture he was painting. Her heart floundered in her chest. What if she couldn't give him what he wanted most?

"I love you too, Nolan," she said choosing to lead with that. "I'm just not sure about having children."

"You don't want kids?" he asked.

"I do." She squeezed out the words through a throat tight with emotion. "Right now all I can think of is watching *our* children run around this porch." Round-faced children with bright blonde hair and their father's blue eyes.

"It'll be great?" He pulled her into a hug. "You've made me the happiest man on the planet, Michelle. And that matters, even when this view makes it look as though we're the only two people in the world."

She chuckled again despite herself. The man had a way. Or maybe she was in shock. Regardless, she had to tell him the truth about the baby she lost. He shouldn't be planning a big-family future with her if she couldn't give him the life of his dreams.

"I miscarried, Nolan," she said. The words seemed to bring the beautiful moment, the world, screeching to a stop. He didn't release her, but his body locked up which was so much worse. "I was pregnant. After that night with you."

"You were *pregnant?*"

The pain in his beautiful eyes knocked her back a step. "I'm sorry." Shame swamped her. It was going to hurt so much when he walked away. Whoever said it was better to love and lose than never love at all was an idiot.

"I'd been planning to call you," she continued. "I'd only known about the baby for a few days when it all fell apart. Afterward…" Her voice trailed off and she struggled to find a shred of courage. "After it happened, I didn't know what to say. There was no need to stress you out or drag you into a situation that had resolved itself."

"So you went through it alone." His voice was as rough as the gravel under their feet. His golden eyebrows furrowed. To her shock he pulled her into his arms. She didn't know what to do. Shouldn't he be pushing her away? "*I'm* sorry. Tell me, now. If you can."

He drew her down to sit with him on the small concrete bench. The story came out of her little by little with the flowers at her back and the sunset painting the horizon. Somehow the fear and the sorry faded as she shared the burden with him. "They think I'm okay, but there's no way to be sure what will happen. I love you. You want a family but I may not be the woman who can give that to you."

"Oh, Michelle. No one ever knows for sure. I'm so sorry you dealt with it all alone. Family is what we say it is." He tipped up her chin to look into her eyes. "I want you first. First and last." He kissed her softly. "I would have been here for you. I want to be here for you for everything still to come. The good and the bad."

She believed him, heart, mind and soul. "You really want to take a chance with me?"

"The way I see it you're the only sure thing," he said. "And our connection, the love I feel for you is so rare. I've watched others find it and I've been jealous. You're special to me, when I'm with you there is just so much hope, so much sunlight.

"I know it hasn't been traditional in any sense, but the history between us is ours. Tell me you'll help me build our future. Right here, where we can both work and grow." He shifted away and pulled something from his pocket. "This is from your shop," he said with an unrepentant grin. "I saw it while the police were taking statements and we were cleaning up and knew it was the right ring for you. For this moment."

"You stole from me." But she couldn't even pretend to be stern while her heart fluttered with happiness.

"Seems only fair since you stole my heart a year ago." He touched his nose to hers. "I'd like to be the only thief in your world from this day forward. Marry me Michelle. For better or worse, let's stop being alone and start really living in love."

"Oh, Nolan. Are you sure?"

"My only regret is not coming home sooner."

"Then, yes. Always, forever, yes." She cradled his face and kissed him, every hope in her heart soaring free under that gorgeous sunset. Soaring free toward a future with the man of her dreams.

Off The Radar

For full details on all of Regan's books visit ReganBlack.com and

enjoy excerpts from each of her sexy, adrenaline-fueled novels.

Black Ice, Book 4 in Stormwatch, a multi-author series

what she knew, Book 4 in Breakdown, a multi-author series

Knight Traveler Series

The Matchmaker Series

Escape Club Heroes, Harlequin Romantic Suspense

The Riley Code, Harlequin Romantic Suspense

Colton Family saga, a multi-author series, Harlequin Romantic Suspense

Regan Black, a USA Today and internationally bestselling author, writes award-winning, action-packed romances featuring kick-butt heroines and the sexy heroes who fall in love with them. Raised in the Midwest and California, she and her husband share their empty nest with two adorably arrogant cats in the South Carolina Lowcountry where the rich blend of legend, romance, and history fuels her imagination.

For early access to new book releases, exclusive prizes, and much more, subscribe to the monthly newsletter at ReganBlack.com/perks.

Keep up with Regan online:
www.ReganBlack.com
Facebook
Twitter
Instagram
Or follow Regan at:

BookBub

Amazon

facebook.com/ReganBlack.fans
twitter.com/ReganBlack
instagram.com/reganblackauthor

BROTHERHOOD PROTECTORS

ORIGINAL SERIES BY ELLE JAMES

ABOUT ELLE JAMES

ELLE JAMES also writing as MYLA JACKSON is a *New York Times* and *USA Today* Bestselling author of books including cowboys, intrigues and paranormal adventures that keep her readers on the edges of their seats. With over eighty works in a variety of sub-genres and lengths she has published with Harlequin, Samhain, Ellora's Cave, Kensington, Cleis Press, and Avon. When she's not at her computer, she's traveling, snow skiing, boating, or riding her ATV, dreaming up new stories. Learn more about Elle James at www.elle-james.com

Website | Facebook | Twitter | GoodReads | Newsletter | BookBub | Amazon

Follow Elle!
www.ellejames.com
ellejames@ellejames.com

facebook.com/ellejamesauthor
twitter.com/ElleJamesAuthor

Printed in the USA
CPSIA information can be obtained
at www.ICGtesting.com
LVHW020205090424
776841LV00028B/745

9 781626 953239